ADAM, ONE AF
and other stories

Italo Calvino was born in Cuba in 1923. He grew up in Italy. He was an essayist and journalist and a member of the editorial staff of Einaudi in Turin. His other novels include *Invisible Cities* and *The Castle of Crossed Destinies*. In 1973 he won the prestigious Premio Feltrinelli. Italo Calvino died in 1985.

ALSO BY ITALO CALVINO

Italo Calvino

ADAM ONE
AFTERNOON
and other stories

Translated by
Archibald Colquhoun and Peggy Wright

VINTAGE

Published by Vintage 2000

3 5 7 9 10 8 6 4

'The Argentine Ant' was first published in *Botteghe Oscure X*
in 1952. The other stories in this book were included in *Ultimo
viene il corvo*, first published by Einaudi in 1949.

First published in Great Britain by Collins 1957

Vintage
Random House, 20 Vauxhall Bridge Road,
London SW1V 2SA

Random House Australia (Pty) Limited
20 Alfred Street, Milsons Point, Sydney,
New South Wales 2061, Australia

Random House New Zealand Limited
18 Poland Road, Glenfield,
Auckland 10, New Zealand

Random House (Pty) Limited
Endulini, 5a Jubilee Road, Parktown 2193, South Africa

The Random House Group Limited Reg. No. 954009
www.randomhouse.co.uk

A CIP catalogue record for this book
is available from the British Library

ISBN 0 09 928703 X

Printed and bound in Great Britain by
Cox & Wyman Ltd, Reading, Berkshire

CONTENTS

CONTENTS

Adam, One Afternoon

THE NEW gardener's boy had long hair which he kept in place by a piece of stuff tied round his head with a little bow. He was walking along the path with his watering-can filled to the brim and his other arm stretched out to balance the load. Slowly, carefully, he watered the nasturtiums as if pouring out coffee and milk, until the earth at the foot of each plant dissolved into a soft black patch; when it was large and moist enough he lifted the watering-can and passed on to the next plant. Maria-nunziata was watching him from the kitchen window, and thinking what a nice calm job gardening must be. He was a grown youth, she noticed, though he still wore shorts and that long hair made him look like a girl. She stopped washing the dishes and tapped on the window.

"Hey, boy," she called.

The gardener's boy raised his head, saw Maria-nunziata and smiled. She laughed back at him, partly because she had never seen a boy with such long hair and a bow like that on his head. The gardener's boy beckoned to her with one hand, and Maria-nunziata went on laughing at the funny gesture he'd made, and began gesturing back to explain that she had the dishes to wash. But the boy beckoned again, and pointed at the pots of dahlias with his other hand. Why was he pointing at those dahlias? Maria-nunziata opened the window and put her head out.

"What's up?" she asked, and began laughing again.

"D'you want to see something nice?"

7

" What's that ? "

" Something nice. Come and see. Quickly."

" Tell me what."

" I'll give you it. I'll give you something very nice."

" But I've the dishes to wash, and the Signora'll come along and not find me."

" Do you want it or don't you? Come on, now."

" Wait a second," said Maria-nunziata, and shut the window. When she came out through the kitchen door the gardener's boy was still there, watering the nasturtiums.

" Hallo," said Maria-nunziata.

Maria-nunziata seemed taller than she was because of her high-heeled shoes, which were a pity to work in, but she loved wearing them. Her little face looked like a child's amid its mass of black curls, and her legs were thin and childlike too, though her body, under the folds of her apron, was already round and ripe. She was always laughing: either at what others or she herself said.

" Hallo," said the gardener's boy. The skin on his face, neck and chest was dark brown; perhaps because he was always half naked, as now.

" What's your name? " asked Maria-nunziata.

" Libereso," said the gardener's boy.

Maria-nunziata laughed and repeated: " Libereso . . . Libereso . . . what a funny name, Libereso."

" It's a name in Esperanto," he said. " In Esperanto it means ' liberty.' "

" Esperanto," said Maria-nunziata. " Are you Esperanto? "

" Esperanto's a language," explained Libereso. " My father speaks Esperanto."

" I'm Calabrian," exclaimed Maria-nunziata.

"What's your name? "

" Maria-nunziata," she said and laughed.

"Why are you always laughing? "

" Why are you called Esperanto? "

" Not Esperanto, Libereso."

" Why? "

" Why are you called Maria-nunziata? "

" It is the Madonna's name. I'm called after the Madonna and my brother after Saint Joseph."

" Senjosef? "

Maria-nunziata burst out laughing: " Senjosef! Saint Joseph, not Senjosef, Libereso! "

" My brother," said Libereso, " is called ' Germinal' and my sister ' Omnia.' "

" That nice thing you mentioned," said Maria-nunziata, " show me it."

" Come on, then," said Libereso. He put down the watering-can and took her by the hand.

Maria-nunziata hesitated. " Tell me what it is first."

" You'll see," he said, " but you must promise me to take care of it."

" Will you give it to me? "

" Yes, I'll give it to you." He had led her to a corner of the garden wall. There the dahlias standing in pots were as tall as themselves.

" It's there."

" What is? "

" Wait."

Maria-nunziata peeped over his shoulder. Libereso bent down to move a pot, lifted another by the wall, and pointed to the ground.

" There," he said.

" What is it? " asked Maria-nunziata. She could not see anything; the corner was in shadow, full of wet leaves and garden mould.

" Look, it's moving," said the boy. Then she saw something which looked like a moving stone or leaf, something wet, with eyes and feet; a toad.

9

" *Mammamia!* "

Maria-nunziata went skipping off among the dahlias in her high heeled shoes. Libereso squatted down by the toad and laughed, showing the white teeth in the middle of his brown face.

" Are you frightened? It's only a toad! Why are you frightened? "

" A toad! " gasped Maria-nunziata.

" Of course it's a toad. Come here, " said Libereso.

She pointed at it with a trembling finger. " Kill it. "

He put out his hands, as if to protect it. " I don't want to. It's so nice. "

" A nice toad? "

" All toads are nice. They eat the worms. "

" Oh! " said Maria-nunziata, but she did not come any nearer. She was chewing the edge of her apron and trying to watch from the corner of her eyes.

" Look how pretty it is, " said Libereso and put a hand on it.

Maria-nunziata approached, no longer laughing, and looked on open mouthed. " No! No! Don't touch it! "

With one finger Libereso was stroking the toad's grey-green back, which was covered with slimy warts.

" Are you mad? Don't you know they burn when you touch them, and make your hand swell up? "

The boy showed her his big brown hands, the palms covered with a layer of yellow callouses.

" Oh, it won't hurt me, " he said. " And it's so pretty. "

Now he'd taken the toad by the scruff of the neck like a cat and put it in the palm of his hand. Maria-nunziata, still chewing the edge of her apron, came nearer and crouched down beside him.

" *Mammamia!* " she exclaimed.

They were both crouching down behind the dahlias, and Maria-nunziata's rosy knees were grazing the brown, scratched ones of Libereso. Libereso cupped his other hand over the back of the toad, and caught it every now and again as it tried to slip out.

" You stroke it, Maria-nunziata," he said.

The girl hid her hands in her apron.

" No," she said firmly.

" What? " he said. " You don't want it? "

Maria-nunziata lowered her eyes, glanced at the toad, and lowered them again quickly.

" No," she said.

" But it's yours. I'm giving it to you," said Libereso.

Maria-nunziata's eyes clouded over. It was sad to refuse a present, no one ever gave her presents, but the toad really did revolt her.

" You can take it home if you like. It'll keep you company."

" No," she said.

Libereso put the toad back on the ground and it quickly hopped off and squatted under the leaves.

" Good-bye, Libereso."

" Wait a minute."

" But I must go and finish washing the dishes. The Signora doesn't like me coming out in the garden."

" Wait. I want to give you something. Something really nice. Come along."

She began following him along the gravel paths. What a strange boy this Libereso was, with that long hair, and picking up toads in his hands.

" How old are you, Libereso? "

" Fifteen. And you? "

" Fourteen."

" Now, or on your next birthday? "

" On my next birthday. Assumption Day."

" Has that passed yet? "

"What, don't you know when Assumption Day is? " She began laughing.

" No."

" Assumption Day, when there's the procession. Don't you go to the procession? "

" Me? No."

" Back home there are lovely processions. It's not like here, back home. There are big fields full of bergamots, nothing but bergamots, and everyone picks bergamots from morning till night. I've fourteen brothers and sisters and they all pick bergamots; five died when they were babies, and then my mother got tetanus, and we were in a train for a week to go to Uncle Carmelo's, and eight of us all slept in a garage there. Tell me, why've you got such long hair? "

They had stopped.

" Because it grows like that. You've got long hair too."

" I'm a girl. If you wear long hair, you're like a girl."

" I'm not like a girl. You don't tell a boy from a girl by the hair."

" Not by the hair? "

"'No, not by the hair."

" Why not by the hair? "

" Would you like me to give you something nice? "

" Oh, yes."

Libereso began moving among the arum lilies, budding white trumpets silhouetted against the sky. Libereso looked into each, groped around with two fingers, and then hid something in his fist. Maria-nunziata had not gone into the flower-bed, and was watching him, with silent laughter. What was he up to now? Libereso had now looked into all the lilies. He came up to her holding one hand over the other.

" Open your hands," he said. Maria-nunziata cupped her hands, but was afraid to put them under his.

" What have you got in there? "

" Something very nice. You'll see."

" Show me, first."

12

Libereso opened his hands and let her look inside. His palm was full of multi-coloured rose-chafers, red and black and even purple ones, but the green were the prettiest. They were buzzing and slithering over each other and waving little black legs in the air. Maria-nunziata hid her hands under her apron.

" Here," said Libereso. " Don't you like them? "

" Yes," said Maria-nunziata uncertainly, still keeping her hands under her apron.

" When you hold them tight they tickle; would you like to feel? "

Maria-nunziata held out her hands timidly, and Libereso poured a cascade of rose-chafers of every colour into them.

" Don't be frightened, they won't bite you."

" *Mammamia!* " It hadn't occurred to her that they might bite her. She opened her hands and the rose-chafers spread their wings and the beautiful colours vanished and there was nothing to be seen but a swarm of black insects flying about and settling.

" What a pity. I try to give you a present and you don't want it."

" I must go and do the washing up. The Signora will be cross if she can't find me."

" Don't you want a present? "

" What are you going to give me now? "

" Come and see."

He took her hand again and led her through the flower-beds.

" I must get back to the kitchen soon, Libereso. There's a chicken to pluck, too."

" Poof! "

" Why poof? "

" We don't eat the flesh of dead birds or animals."

" Why, are you always in Lent? "

" What do you mean? "

" Well, what do you eat then? "

" Oh, all sorts of things, artichokes, lettuces, tomatoes. My father doesn't like us to eat the flesh of dead animals. Or coffee or sugar, either."

"What d'you do with your sugar ration, then?"

"Sell it on the black market."

They had reached some climbing plants, starred all over with red flowers.

"What lovely flowers," said Maria-nunziata. "D'you ever pick them?"

"What for?"

"To take to the Madonna. Flowers are for the Madonna."

"Mesembryanthemum."

"What's that?"

"This plant's called Mesembryanthemum in Latin. All flowers have Latin names."

"The Mass is in Latin, too."

"I don't know about that."

Libereso was now peering closely between the winding branches on the wall.

"There it is," he said.

"What is?"

It was a lizard green with black markings, basking in the sun.

"I'll catch it."

"No."

But he got closer to the lizard, very slowly, with both hands open; a jump, and he'd caught it. He laughed happily, showing his white teeth. "Look out, it's escaping!" First a stunned-looking head, then a tail, slithered out between his closed fingers. Maria-nunziata was laughing too, but every time she saw the lizard she skipped back and pulled her skirt tight about her knees.

"So you really don't want me to give you anything at all?" said Libereso, rather sadly, and very carefully he put the lizard back on the wall; off it shot. Maria-nunziata kept her eyes lowered.

" Come along," said Libereso, and took her hand again.

" I'd like to have a lipstick and paint my lips red on Sundays to go out dancing. And a black veil to put on my head afterwards for Benediction."

" On Sundays," said Libereso, " I go to the woods with my brother and we fill two sacks with pine cones. Then, in the evening, my father reads out loud from Kropotkin. My father has hair down to his shoulders and a beard right down to his chest. And he wears shorts in summer and winter. And I do drawings for the Anarchist Federation windows. The figures in top hats are business men, those in caps are generals, and those in round hats are priests; then I paint them in water colours."

They came to a pond with round water-lily leaves floating on it.

" Quiet, now," commanded Libereso.

Under the water a frog could be seen swimming up with sharp little strokes of its green arms and legs. It suddenly surfaced, jumped on to a water-lily leaf and sat down in the middle.

" There," cried Libereso and put out a hand to catch it, but Maria-nunziata let out a cry, " Uh ! " and the frog jumped back into the water. Libereso began searching for it, his nose almost touching the surface.

" There it is."

He thrust in a hand and pulled it out in his closed fist.

" Two of them together," he cried. " Look. Two of them, on top of each other."

" Why ? " asked Maria-nunziata.

" Male and female stuck together," said Libereso. " Look what they are doing." And he tried to put the frogs into Maria-nunziata's hand. Maria-nunziata wasn't sure if she was frightened because they were frogs, or because they were male and female stuck together.

" Leave them alone," she said. " You mustn't touch them."

" Male and female," repeated Libereso. " They're making

tadpoles." A cloud passed over the sun. Suddenly Maria-nunziata began to feel anxious.

"It's late. The Signora's sure to be looking for me."

But she did not go. Instead they went on wandering around though the sun did not come out again. And then he found a snake: it was a tiny little snake behind a hedge of bamboo. Libereso wound it round his arm and stroked its head.

"Once I used to train snakes. I had a dozen of them, one was long and yellow, a water snake. But it shed its skin and escaped. Look at this one opening its mouth, look how its tongue is forked. Stroke it, it won't bite."

But Maria-nunziata was frightened of snakes too. Then they went to the rock pool. First he showed her the fountains, and opened all the jets, which pleased her very much. Then he showed her the goldfish. It was a lonely old goldfish, and its scales were already whitening. At last; Maria-nunziata liked the goldfish. Libereso began to move his hands round in the water to catch it; it was very difficult, but when he'd caught it Maria-nunziata could put it in a bowl and keep it in the kitchen. He managed to catch it, but didn't take it out of the water in case it suffocated.

"Put your hands down here, stroke it," said Libereso. "You can feel it breathing; it has fins like paper and scales that prickle. not much though."

But Maria-nunziata did not want to stroke the fish either.

In the petunia bed the earth was very soft, and Libereso dug about with his fingers and pulled out some long, soft worms.

But Maria-nunziata ran away with little shrieks.

"Put your hand here," said Libereso, pointing to the trunk of an old peach tree. Maria-nunziata did not understand why, but she put her hand there; then she screamed and ran to dip it in the pool. For when she had pulled her hand away it was covered with ants. The peach tree was a mass of them, tiny black "Argentine" ants.

"Look," said Libereso and put a hand on the trunk. The ants

16

could be seen crawling over his hand but he didn't brush them off.

"Why?" asked Maria-nunziata. "Why are you letting yourself get covered with ants?"

His hand was now quite black, and they were crawling up his wrist.

"Take your hand away," moaned Maria-nunziata. "You'll get them all over you."

The ants were crawling up his naked arm, and had already reached his elbow.

Now his whole arm was covered with a veil of moving black dots; they reached his armpit but he did not brush them off.

"Get rid of them, Libereso. Put your arm in water!"

Libereso laughed, some ants now even crawling from his neck on to his face.

"Libereso! I'll do whatever you like! I'll accept all those presents you gave me."

She threw her arms round his neck and started to brush off the ants.

Smiling his brown and white smile, Libereso took his hand away from the tree and began nonchalantly dusting his arm. But he was obviously touched.

"Very well, then, I'll give you a really big present, I've decided. The biggest present I can."

"What's that?"

"A hedgehog."

"*Mammamia!* The Signora! The Signora's calling me!"

Maria-nunziata had just finished washing the dishes when she heard a pebble beat against the window. Underneath stood Libereso with a large basket.

"Maria-nunziata, let me in. I want to give you a surprise."

"No, you can't come up. What have you got there?"

But at that moment the Signora rang the bell, and Maria-nunziata vanished.

When she returned to the kitchen, Libereso was no longer to be seen. Neither inside the kitchen or underneath the window. Maria-nunziata went up to the sink. Then she saw the surprise.

On every plate she had left to dry there was a crouching frog; a snake was coiled up inside a saucepan, there was a soup bowl full of lizards, and slimy snails were making iridescent streaks all over the glasses. In the basin full of water swam the lonely old goldfish.

Maria-nunziata stepped back, but between her feet she saw a great big toad. And behind it were five little toads in a line, taking little hops towards her across the black and white tiled floor.

The Enchanted Garden

GIOVANNINO AND Serenella were strolling along the railway lines. Below was a scaly sea of sombre, clear blue; above, a sky lightly streaked with white clouds. The railway lines were shimmering and burning hot. It was fun going along the railway, there were so many games to play—he balancing on one rail holding her hand while she walked along on the other, or else both jumping from one sleeper to the next without ever letting their feet touch the stones in between. Giovannino and Serenella had been out looking for crabs, and now they had decided to explore the railway lines as far as the tunnel. He liked playing with Serenella, as she did not behave as all the other little girls did, for ever getting frightened or bursting into tears at every joke. Whenever Giovannino said " Let's go there," or " Let's do this," Serenella always followed without a word.

Ping! They both gave a start and looked up. A telephone wire had snapped off the top of the pole. It sounded like an iron stork suddenly shutting its beak. They stood with their noses in the air and watched. What a pity not to have seen it! Now, it would never happen again.

" There's a train coming," said Giovannino.

Serenella did not move from the rail. "Where from?" she asked.

Giovannino looked round in a knowledgeable way. He pointed at the black hole of the tunnel which showed clear one moment, then misty the next, through the invisible heat haze rising from the stony track.

"From there," he said. They already seemed to hear a snort from the darkness of the tunnel, and see the train suddenly appear belching out fire and smoke, the wheels mercilessly eating up the rails as it hurtled towards them.

"Where shall we go, Giovannino?"

There were big grey aloes down towards the sea, surrounded by dense impenetrable nettles, while up the hillside ran a rambling hedge with thick leaves but no flowers. There was no sign of the train still; perhaps it was running on with the engine cut off, and would jump out at them all of a sudden. But Giovannino had now found an opening in the hedge. "This way," he called.

The fence under the rambling hedge was an old bent rail. At one point it twisted about on the ground like the corner of a sheet of paper. Giovannino had slipped into the hole and already half vanished.

"Give me a hand, Giovannino."

They found themselves in a corner of a garden, on all fours in a flower-bed, with their hair full of dry leaves and moss. Everything was quiet; not a leaf was stirring.

"Come on," said Giovannino, and Serenella nodded in reply.

There were big, old, flesh-coloured eucalyptus trees and winding gravel paths. Giovannino and Serenella tiptoed along the paths, taking care not to crunch the gravel. Suppose the owners appeared now?

Everything was so beautiful: narrow turnings and high, curling eucalyptus leaves and patches of sky; but there was always the worrying thought that it was not their garden, and that they might be chased away any moment. But not a sound could be heard. A flight of chattering sparrows rose from a clump of arbutus at a turn in the path. Then all was silent again. Perhaps it was an abandoned garden?

But the shade of the big trees came to an end, and they found themselves under the open sky facing flower-beds filled with neat rows of petunias and convolvulus, and paths and balustrades and rows of box trees. And up at the end of the garden was a large villa with flashing window panes and yellow and orange curtains.

And it was all quite deserted. The two children crept forward treading carefully over the gravel: perhaps the windows would be suddenly flung open, and angry ladies and gentlemen appear on the terraces and unleash great dogs down the paths. They now found a wheelbarrow standing near a ditch. Giovannino took it up by the handles and began pushing it along in front of him: it creaked like a whistle at every turn. Serenella sat herself in it and they moved slowly forward, Giovannino pushing the barrow with her on top, along the flower beds and fountains.

Every now and then Serenella would point to a flower and say in a low voice, "That one," and Giovannino would put the barrow down, pluck it, and give it to her. Soon she had a lovely bunch of flowers.

Eventually the gravel ended and they reached an open space paved in bricks and mortar. And in the middle of this space was a big empty rectangle: a swimming pool. They crept up to the edge: it was lined with blue tiles and filled to the brim with clear water. How lovely it would be to bathe in!

"Shall we have a dip?" Giovannino asked Serenella. The idea must have been quite dangerous if he asked her instead of just saying, "In we go!" But the water was so clear and blue, and Serenella was never frightened. She jumped off the barrow and put her bunch of flowers in it. They were already in bathing dresses, as they'd been out for crabs till just before. Giovannino plunged in; not from the diving board, as the splash would have made too much noise, but from the edge of the pool. Down and down he went with his eyes wide open, seeing only the blue from the tiles and his pink hands like goldfish; it was not the same as under the sea, full of shapeless green-black shadows. A pink form appeared above him: Serenella! He took her hand

21

and they swam up to the surface, rather anxiously. No, there was no one watching them at all. But it was not so nice as they'd thought it would be; they always had that uncomfortable feeling that they had no right to any of this, and might be chased out at any moment.

They scrambled out of the water, and there beside the swimming pool they found a ping-pong table. Giovannino at once picked up the bat and hit the ball, and Serenella, on the other side, was quick to return the shot. And so they went on playing, giving only light taps at the ball, though, in case someone in the villa heard them. But then Giovannino, in trying to parry a shot that bounced high, sent the ball sailing away through the air and smack against a gong hanging in a pergola. There was a long, sombre boom. The two children crouched down behind a clump of ranunculus. And at once two men-servants in white coats appeared, carrying big trays; they put the trays down on a round table under an orange and yellow striped umbrella, and off they went.

Giovannino and Serenella crept up to the table. There was tea, milk and sponge cake. They had only to sit down and help themselves. They poured out two cups of tea and cut two slices of cake. But somehow they did not feel at all at ease, and sat perched on the edge of their chairs, moving their knees. And they could not really enjoy the tea and cakes, as nothing seemed to have any taste. Everything in the garden was like that: lovely but impossible to enjoy properly, with that worrying feeling inside that they were only there from an odd stroke of luck, and the fear that they'd soon have to give an account of themselves.

Very quietly they tiptoed up to the villa. Between the slits of a venetian blind they saw a beautiful shady room, with collections of butterflies hanging on the walls. And in the room was a pale little boy. Lucky boy, he must be the owner of this villa and garden. He was lying stretched on a long chair, turning over the pages of a large book filled with figures. He had big white hands and wore pyjamas buttoned up to the neck, though it was summer.

Now as the two children went on peeping through the slits the pounding of their hearts gradually subsided. Why, the little rich boy seemed to be sitting there and turning over the pages and glancing round with more anxiety and worry than their own. And then he got up and tiptoed round, as if he were afraid that at any moment someone would come and turn him out, as if he felt that book, that long chair and those butterflies framed on the wall, the garden and games and tea trays, the swimming pool and paths, were only granted to him by some enormous mistake, as if he were incapable of enjoying them and felt the bitterness of the mistake as his own fault.

The pale boy was wandering round his shady room with furtive steps, touching with his white fingers the edges of the cases studded with butterflies; then he stopped to listen. The pounding of Giovannino and Serenella's hearts, which had died down, now began harder than ever. Perhaps it was the fear of a spell which hung over this villa and garden and over all these lovely comfortable things, like some ancient injustice committed long ago.

Clouds darkened the sun. Very quietly Giovannino and Serenella crept away. They went back along the same paths they had come, stepping fast but never at a run. And they went through the hedge again on all fours. Between the aloes they found a path leading down to the small, stony beach, with banks of seaweed along the shore. Then they invented a wonderful new game; a seaweed fight. They threw great handfuls of it in each other's faces till late in the afternoon. And Serenella never once cried.

Father to Son

OXEN ARE scarce, in our parts. There are no meadows for pasture, or big fields to plough; only fruit trees and short strips of earth so hard it has to be broken by hoe. And anyway oxen and cows would be out of place here, too big and placid for our narrow craggy valleys; to clamber among these rocks animals here must be thin and gristly; mules and goats, for instance.

The Scarassas' ox was the only one in the valley; it did not seem out of place though, for it was a sturdy little pack animal, stronger and more docile than any mule. Moretobello, it was called. It earned a living for the two Scarassas, father and son, by journeying about for the various landowners in the valley, with sacks of corn for the mill, or palm leaves for the exporters, or manure for the syndicate.

Moretobello was lurching along, that day, under a load balanced on both sides of the pack saddle: olive logs to be sold to a client in the town. The rope drooping from the ring in its soft black nostrils almost touched the ground, before ending in the dangling hands of Nanin, Battistin Scarassa's son, as lank and haggard as his father; Scarassa, in fact, was a nickname which meant vine-pole. They were an odd couple: the ox, with its short legs and its broad low toad-like belly, stepping carefully along under its burden; Scarassa, his long face bristling with red stubble, his wrists sticking out of his short sleeves, kicking out at each step from apparently

24

double jointed knees, while his trousers fluttered like sails at every gust of wind as if there were nothing inside them.

Spring was in the air that morning; there was that sense of re-discovery, that is, which comes all of a sudden one morning every year, a reminder of something that had seemed forgotten for months. Moretobello, usually so calm, was restless. Earlier that morning Nanin had not found it in its stall when he went to fetch it; it had been out in the field, its eyes rolling and lost. Now Moretobello was stopping every now and again as it went along, raising its nostrils pierced by the ring, and sniffing the air with a short bellow. Then Nanin would give a yank at the rope and a gutteral call in the language men use to oxen.

Some thought seemed to be striking Moretobello every now and again; it had had a dream, that night, which was why it had left the stall and felt lost to the world that morning: a dream of forgotten things which seemed to come from another life; of wide grassy plains filled with cows, endless cows, coming lowing towards it. And it had seen itself, there in the middle of them, running about in the herd of cows as if looking for something. But it was held back, prevented from contact with the herd by a red hook sticking in its flesh. And that morning, as Moretobello lurched along, it could still feel the wound made by that red hook.

On their way they kept on meeting little boys in white suits with gold-fringed bands on their arms, and little girls dressed up as brides; it was First Communion Day. Whenever Nanin saw them something seemed to darken in the bottom of his mind, a kind of old nagging resentment. Perhaps it was the knowledge that his own children would never have any of those white clothes to wear for First Communion. What a lot they must cost! Then he felt a raging longing to have his children confirmed come over him. Already he could see his little son dressed up in a white sailor suit with a gold-fringed band on his arm, his little daughter in veil and train, amid the glimmering shadows of the church.

The ox gave a snort; it was remembering its dream, seeing the herd of cows galloping along, as if in some area outside its memory, with itself among them straining more and more to keep up. Suddenly a great bull appeared on a mound in the middle of the herd; it was red like the pain of that wound, its horns were like scythes touching the sky, and it charged at Moretobello with a roar.

On the little square in front of the church the children on their way to Confirmation began running around the ox. "An ox! An ox!" they shouted. It was an unusual sight, an ox was, in those parts. The bravest were even daring to touch its belly, while the most knowing cried: "It's a bullock! Look, it's a bullock!" Nanin shouted and waved his fists about to send them away. Then the children began making fun of him for being so thin, haggard and ragged, and jeering out his nickname: "Scarassa! Scarassa!"

Nanin felt that nagging old resentment of his getting stronger, more agonising. He remembered other children dressed for First Communion jeering not at him but at his father, thin, haggard and ragged as he was himself now, the day he had been taken to First Communion when a child. And there returned, sharp as ever, the pang of shame he had felt for his father at seeing the children jumping round him, flinging rose petals that had been trodden in the procession and shouting "Scarassa!" That shame had been with him all his life, made him resent every look, every laugh. And it had all been his father's fault; what had he ever inherited from him but squalor, stupidity, the clumsy movements of his lanky body? He hated his father, he suddenly realised, for the shame he had made him feel as a boy, for the shame and squalor of his whole life. And now a fear was coming over him that his own children would be as ashamed of him as he was of his father, and look at him one day with the same hatred he had in his eyes now. And he decided: "I'll buy myself a new suit for their First Communion; of checked flannel. And a white linen cap. And

26

a coloured tie. And my wife must buy herself a new woollen dress too, big enough to wear when she's pregnant. And we'll walk together, all nicely dressed, to the church square. And buy ices from the ice-cream cart." But even after they'd bought the ices, after they'd walked round in their best clothes, there was still a yearning in him which he did not know how to satisfy, a yearning to do something, to spend money, to show off, to make up for that shame which had gone with him through life since he was a child.

On reaching home he led the ox to the stall and took off its pack-saddle. Then he went to eat; his wife, the children, and old Battistin were already at table munching bean soup. Old Scarassa, Battistin, was fishing the beans out in his fingers, sucking at them and throwing away the skins. Nanin paid no attention to their talk.

" The children must be confirmed," he said. His wife raised her tired face and uncombed hair towards him.

" And the money for their clothes ? "

" They must have some nice clothes," went on Nanin without looking at her. " The boy a white sailor's suit, with a gold-fringed arm band, the girl a bridal dress, with train and veil."

The wife and the old man looked at him open-mouthed.

" The money ? " they repeated.

" And I'll get myself a check flannel suit," went on Nanin. " And you a woollen dress, big enough to wear when you're pregnant too."

An idea occurred to his wife. " Ah ! You've found someone to buy the Gozzo land."

This was a patch of inherited land, all stones and bushes, which earned them nothing but taxes to pay. It annoyed Nanin they should think that; what he was saying was absurd, but he went on insistently, furiously.

" No, I've not found anyone. But we must have all that," he went on stubbornly, without taking his eyes from his plate. The

27

others were all hopeful now, though; if he'd found someone to buy the Gozzo land, it was all possible.

"With the money from that land," said old Battistin, "I can have my hernia operation."

Nanin felt a stab of hatred for him.

"May it kill you off, you and your hernia!"

The others were now watching to see if he'd gone crazy.

Meanwhile, in the stall, Moretobello the ox had worked itself loose from its rope, burst open the door, and came out into the field. Suddenly it appeared in the room, stopped, and gave out a long, wailing, desperate bellow. Nanin cursed, got up and beat it back into its stall.

When he came in again everyone was silent, even the children. Then the little boy asked: "Daddy, when will you buy me that sailor suit?"

Nanin raised his eyes to him that were exactly like his father, Battistin's.

"Never!" he yelled.

He banged the door and went off to bed.

A Goatherd at Luncheon

IT WAS, as usual, a mistake of my father's. He had had a boy sent down from a village in the mountains to look after our goats. And the day the boy arrived my father insisted on asking him to eat with us.

My father does not understand the things which divide people, the difference between a dining-room like ours, with its inlaid furniture, dark-patterned carpets, majolica plates, and those homes of theirs with smoky stone walls, beaten earth floors, and newspapers black with flies draped over the chimney pieces. My father always goes about among them with that jolly ceremonious air of his, and when they invite him to eat when he is out shooting, as they all do, he insists on eating off the same dirty dish; then in the evening they all come to him to settle their disputes. We, his own sons, don't take much part, though. Perhaps my brother, with that air of silent complicity he has, may occasionally be given some rough confidence; but I'm too well aware of the difficulties of communication between human beings, and sense at every minute the gulfs that separate the classes, the abysses that politeness opens under me.

When the boy came in, I was reading a paper. My father began fussing over him—what was the point?—he'd only get all the more confused. But he didn't. I raised my eyes and there he was in the middle of the room, with his heavy hands and his chin on his chest, but looking straight ahead of him, stubbornly. He was a goatherd boy of my own age, about, with compact, wooden-looking hair, and high features—forehead, nose, cheeks. He wore a dark military shirt with its top button straining over his Adam's apple, and a crumpled old suit from which the big knobbly hands and the great boots, lifting slowly on the gleaming floor, seemed like an overflow.

" This is my son Quinto," said my father. " He's at high school."

I got up and put on a smile; my outstretched hand met his and we immediately moved away without looking the other in the face. My father had already begun saying things about me that no one could want to hear, how long I still had at school, how I'd once killed a squirrel out shooting in the part the shepherd came from; and I kept on shrugging my shoulders as if to say: " Me? Really, no!" The goatherd stood there mute and still, showing no sign of following; every now and again he gave a quick glance towards one of the walls or curtains, like an animal looking for an opening in a cage.

Then my father changed the subject and began walking round the room talking about certain varieties of vegetables grown up in those valleys. He kept asking the boy questions, while the goatherd, with his chin on his chest and his mouth half shut, kept on saying he did not know. Hidden behind the newspaper, I waited for the food to be served. But my father had already made his guest sit down, and brought him a cucumber from the kitchen and began cutting it up into his soup plate in small pieces, for him to eat as hors d'œuvre, he told him.

Now my mother came in, tall, dressed in black with lace trimmings, her smooth white hair rigidly parted. " Ah, here's our little goatherd boy," she said. " Have you had a good journey?" The boy did not get up or reply, but just raised his eyes to my mother in a look full of uncomprehending distrust. I felt whole-heartedly on his side; I disapproved of the tone of affectionate superiority my mother was using; I even found myself preferring my father's manner, his rather servile affability, to her aristocratic

30

condescension. And then I hated that possessive " *tu* " by which my mother addressed the boy; if she'd been using dialect like my father it might have been all right, but she was talking Italian to the poor goatherd, an Italian cold as a marble wall.

To protect him I tried to turn the conversation away from him. So I read out an item of news from the paper, something which could only interest my parents, about a vein of mineral ore discovered in a part of Africa where certain friends of ours lived. I had chosen on purpose an item of news which could have no conceivable connection with the guest, and which was full of names unknown to him; and I did this not to make his isolation weigh on him more, but so as to dig a ditch round him, as it were, give him a breathing space and distract my parents' besieging attentions for a moment. Perhaps he, too, interpreted my move wrongly. Anyway, its effect was contrary. My father began to ramble on with a story about Africa, confusing the boy with a tangle of strange names of places, peoples, and animals.

Just as the soup was being served my grandmother appeared in her wheel chair, pushed by my poor sister Cristina. They had to shout loudly in her ear to tell her what was happening. My mother, indeed, made a formal introduction: " This is Giovannino, who is going to look after our goats. My mother. My daughter Cristina."

I blushed with shame at hearing him called Giovannino, little Giovannino; how different that name must have sounded in the closed rough dialect of the mountains; certainly it was the first time he heard himself called it in that way.

My grandmother nodded with patriarchal calm: " Fine, Giovannino, let's hope you don't let any goats escape, eh!" My sister Cristina, who treats all our rare visitors as people of great distinction, now muttered " Delighted " in a terrified way, half-hidden behind the back of the wheel chair, and she held her hand out to the youth, who shook it heavily.

The goatherd was sitting on the edge of his chair, but with his shoulders back and his hands spread on the tablecloth, looking at my grandmother as if fascinated. The old woman was sunk in her big arm-chair, with mittens half covering bloodless fingers making vague movements in the air, a tiny face under its network of wrinkles, spectacles turned towards him trying to make out some shape in the confused mass of shadows and colours transmitted by her eyes, and speaking an Italian which sounded as if she were reading out of a book. It must all have seemed so different to him from the other old women he had met, that perhaps he thought he was face to face with a new species of human being.

My poor sister Cristina had not moved from her corner. As usual when she saw a new face, she now advanced into the middle of the room, her hands joined under the little shawl drawn over her deformed shoulders, her head streaked with premature grey, her face marked with the boredom of her recluse's life. Raising her clear eyes towards the windows she said: "There's a little boat on the sea, I've seen it. And two sailors rowing on and on. And then it passed behind the roof of a house and no one saw it any more."

I wanted our guest to realise my sister's unfortunate state at once, so that he should take no more notice of her. I jumped up, and with a forced animation which was quite out of place, exclaimed: "But how can you have seen men in a boat from our windows? We're too far away."

My sister went on looking out of the window, not at the sea, though, but at the sky. "Two men in a boat. Rowing on and on. And there was a flag, too, the tricolour flag."

Then I realised that as the shepherd listened to my sister he did not seem as uneasy and out of place as he seemed to be in the presence of all the others. Perhaps he had finally found something that came into his experience, a point of contact between our and his world. And I remembered the idiots who are often to be met in mountain villages, and who spend their hours sitting on thresholds amid clouds of flies, and sadden the village nights with their wails.

Perhaps this family misfortune of ours, which he understood because it was well known to his own people, brought him closer to us than my father's eccentric jollity, the women's maternal and protective airs, and my own awkward detachment.

My brother arrived late as usual, when we already had spoons in our hands. He came in and took in everything at a glance; before my father had explained and introduced him as " My son Marco who's studying to be a notary," he had already sat down to eat, without blinking an eyelid, without looking at anyone. His cold spectacles were so impenetrable they seemed black, his depressing little beard stood out spruce and stiff. He gave the impression of having greeted everyone and excused himself for being late, and even perhaps of having given a smile at the guest, instead of which he had not opened his mouth or wrinkled his smooth forehead with a single line. Now I knew that the goatherd had a powerful ally on his side, an ally who would protect him and make every retreat possible for him by the atmosphere heavy with awkwardness which only he, Marco, knew how to create.

The shepherd was eating, bent over his plate of soup, rinsing it noisily about in his mouth. Now we three males were with him in leaving obvious manners to the women: my father from natural expansive noisiness, my brother from imperious determination, I from ill grace. I was pleased with this new alliance, this rebellion of us four against the women. Certainly the women disapproved of us all at that moment, and avoided saying so only in order not to humiliate us members of the family in front of the guest, and vice versa. But did the shepherd realise this? Definitely not.

My mother now went into the attack, with a very sweet: " And how old are you, Giovannino?"

The boy gave a number which rang out like a shout. He repeated it slowly. " What's that?" said our grandmother and repeated it wrongly. " No, this," and everyone began shouting it in her ear. Only my brother was silent. "A year older than Quinto," my mother now discovered; and this had to be repeated all over again to my grandmother. These were the things I could not bear, which shamed me to the bottom of my heart, for my sake and his; this comparing of him and me, he who had to look after goats to make a living and stank of ram and was strong enough to fell an oak, and I who spent my life on a sofa by the radio reading opera librettos, who would soon be going to the university and disliked flannel next my skin because it made my back prickle. This injustice, these things lacking in me to be him and lacking in him to be me, gave me a sharp feeling of our being, he and I, two incomplete creatures hiding, diffident and ashamed, behind that soup-bowl.

It was then that our grandmother asked: "And have you already done your military service?" This question was ridiculous; his class had not yet been called, he had scarcely passed his first check-up. "A soldier of the Pope," said my father, one of those jokes of his which no one understood and which he had to repeat twice. "They've made me 'returnable,'" said the shepherd. "Oh," said our grandmother, "refused"; and her voice expressed disapproval and regret. Even if he is, I thought, why make so much of it? "No. 'Returnable.'" "And what does that mean: 'Returnable'?" This had to be explained. "Soldier of the Pope, ha ha! Soldier of the Pope," my father laughed. "Oh, I hope you aren't ill," said my mother. "Ill on the day of the medical," said the shepherd, and luckily my grandmother did not hear.

My brother raised his head from the plate then and through his spectacles gave the guest almost a direct glance, a glance of complicity, while his little beard moved slightly at the corners of his lips in a hint of a smile as if to say: "Let the others be, I understand you and know all about these things." It was with these unexpected signals of complicity that Marco attracted sympathy; from now on the shepherd would always turn to him and answer

34

questions every time with a glance in his direction. And yet I guessed that at the roots of this apparent shy humanity of my brother Marco's there lay both the servility of our father and the aristocratic superiority of our mother. And I thought that by allying himself with him the shepherd would not be any less alone.

At this point I thought of something to say that might perhaps interest him; and I explained that I had had my military service deferred until the end of my studies. But now I had brought out the tremendous difference between us two: the impossibility of a common link even about things which seemed everyone's fate, like military service.

My sister now came out with one of her remarks: " And will you go into the Cavalry, sir, excuse me? " This would have passed unobserved if my grandmother had not taken up the subject. " Ah, the Cavalry nowadays . . ." The shepherd muttered something about "Alpini . . ." We realised, I and my brother, that we had at that moment an ally in our mother, who certainly found this subject silly. But why did she not intervene, then, to change the conversation? Luckily my father had stopped repeating: " Ah, a soldier of the Pope . . ." and now asked if mushrooms were growing in the woods.

So we went on for the whole length of the meal, with us three poor boys fighting our war against a cruel torturing world without being able to recognise each other as allies, full of mutual fears. My brother ended by making a great gesture, after the fruit; he took out a packet of cigarettes and offered one to our guest. They lit up without asking if they disturbed anyone; and this was the fullest moment of solidarity created during that meal. I was excluded because my parents did not allow me to smoke till I left school. My brother was satisfied now; he got up, inhaled once or twice, looking down at us, then turned round and went out as silently as he had come.

My father lit his pipe and turned on the wireless for the news.

The goatherd was looking at the instrument with his hands open on his knees and his eyes staring and reddening with tears. Certainly those eyes were still seeing his village high above the fields, the lines of mountains and the thick chestnut woods. My father did not allow us to listen to the wireless, he was criticising the United Nations, and I took advantage of this to leave the dining-room.

That whole afternoon and evening we were persecuted by the memory of the goatherd. We had supper in silence by the dim light of the chandelier and could not free ourselves of the thought of him alone in the hut on our land. Now he must have finished the soup in the can in which he had heated it up, and was lying on the straw almost in the dark, while down below the goats could be heard moving about and bumping each other and munching grass. The goatherd would go outside and there would be a slight mist over towards the sea and damp air and a little spring gurgling gently in the silence. The goatherd would go towards it along paths covered with wild ivy, and drink, though he was not thirsty. Fireflies could be seen appearing and vanishing in what seemed like a great compact swarm. But he would move his arm in the air without touching them.

Leaving Again Shortly

FOR MONTHS, sometimes for years, I'm away from home. Every now and again I return and there my home always is, at the top of the hill, its old red walls standing out amid the thick smokiness of the olives. It's an old house, with ceilings arched like bridges, and masonic symbols on the walls put there by my people in the past to chase away the priests. My brother is always travelling too, but he comes back more often than I do, and when I return I always find him here. As soon as he gets back he looks round till he finds his shooting jacket, his homespun jerkin, and his leather-seated trousers, then he chooses the pipe which draws best, and settles down to a smoke.

" Oh," he exclaims when I arrive, though it may be years since we've seen each other, and he has not expected me. " Hallo," I say, and this is not because there is any coolness between us, for if we met elsewhere we'd make a great fuss and clap each other on the back. "Well ! Well ! " we'd say.

But at home it's different, at home we've always behaved like this.

Then we enter the house, both with our hands in our pockets, silent, a little embarrassed, and all of a sudden my brother begins to talk as if we had just that moment interrupted a conversation.

" Last night," he said, " Giacinto's son nearly came to a bad end."

" You should have shot him, you should," I say, though I don't

37

know what he's talking about. And yet we long to ask each other where we've come from, what jobs we're doing, if we're earning good money, if we're married; but there's time to ask all that afterwards—it would be against our custom to do so now.

"D'you know that Friday night is our turn for using the water at the Long Well?" he says.

"Friday night, to be sure," I repeat, though I don't remember and perhaps have never known.

"D'you think we get the water turned our way every Friday night?" he says. "They'll turn it in theirs if we're not there to watch. Last night I passed by at about eleven, and saw someone running off with a spade in his hand; the channel had been deflected into Giacinto's place."

"You should have shot him, that's what you should have done," I say, already boiling with rage; for months and months I had forgotten all about the question of the Long Well water; in a week I'll be leaving and will forget all about it again; yet now I'm boiling with rage because of the water that's been stolen in the last few months and will be stolen in the next.

Meanwhile, with my brother behind puffing at his pipe, I wander round the stairs and rooms, hung with guns old and new, powder flasks, hunting horns and deers' masks. The stairs and rooms smell musty and moth-eaten, with those masonic symbols everywhere instead of crucifixes. My brother tells me about the labourers' thefts, the ruined crops, the neighbours' goats pasturing in our meadows, the wood gathered by the whole valley from our copses. And I go round the cupboards pulling out jerkins, leggings, coats hung with long pockets for cartridges, and take off my soiled town clothes and look at myself in the mirrors, covered from head to foot in leather and homespun.

A little while later we go wandering down the mule path with shot guns slung over our shoulders, to take a shot at any flying or sitting birds we happen to see. But before we have gone a hundred yards we are caught in the neck by a hail of stones, flung hard, probably from a sling. Instead of turning round at once, we pretend not to notice anything and go on, keeping an eye on the vineyard wall above the path. And there, peeping out among the leaves grey with sulphur spray, is the face of a little boy, a round red face with freckles clustering under the eyes, like a peach eaten by insects.

"By God, they're even setting the children against us!" I say, and begin cursing them.

The boy looks out again, puts out his tongue and runs away. My brother hurries through the vineyard gate and begins running after him down the rows of vines, kicking up the crops, with me behind. Finally we catch him between us. My brother grabs him by the hair, I by the ears, and pull hard, though I know I'm hurting him; but the more I hurt him the angrier I feel. We shout: "That's for you and the rest will be for your father who sent you."

The boy sobs, then bites one of my fingers and escapes. Deep among the vines appears a dark woman hiding the boy's head in the folds of her apron; she begins shouting at us, waving a fist.

"Cowards! To take it out on a child! Always the same bullies! You'll get paid back, don't you worry."

But one doesn't answer women, and we go on our way shrugging our shoulders.

Next we meet two men loaded with bundles of sticks coming towards us, bent double under the weight.

"Hey, you two," we stop them. "Where did you get that wood?"

"Wherever we felt like," they say, and try to move on.

"If you've got it from our woods we'll make you take it back, and what's more we'll string you up on the trees."

The two men have put their loads down on a little wall and are looking at us with sweaty faces from under the sacking protecting their heads and shoulders.

"What's yours and what's not yours is no business of ours. We don't know you."

They do in fact seem to be new people, perhaps unemployed gathering wood on their own. All the more reason to make ourselves known.

" We're the Bagnasco brothers. Ever heard of them?"

" We know nothing about anyone. We got this from the Commune's woods."

" It's forbidden in the Commune's woods. We'll call a guard and have you put inside."

" All right, we do know who you are," one of them suddenly says. " We can't avoid it, you're always having at the poor. But you'll get it one day!"

I begin: " Get what?" then we decide to drop the subject and go off, swearing at each other.

Now, when we're in some other place, my brother and I, we talk to the tram drivers and vendors, give anyone a pull at a cigarette who asks for it, even ask for a pull ourselves sometimes. Here it's different, here we have always behaved like this, going round with our shot guns and having rows everywhere.

At the tavern on the pass there's the local communists' place; hanging outside is a board with newspaper clippings and notices stuck up with pins. As we pass we see a poem tacked up about how the land owners are always the same, and those who were overbearing in the past are the brothers of those who are over-bearing now. " Brothers " is under lined because all this has a double meaning directed against us. We write " Swine and liars " on the sheet of paper; and then sign " Bagnasco Giacomo and Bagnasco Michele."

And yet when we are away we eat at tables covered with chilly wax cloths where other men working away from home eat, and scoop out the soft part of the sticky grey bread; and our neighbour at table talks about the news in the paper, and we too say: " There are still overbearing people about. But one day things'll improve." We couldn't do that here. Here there's land that doesn't produce, labourers who steal and sleep at their work, people who spit behind us when we pass because they don't want to work our land, as all we do, they say, is exploit others.

We reach a spot where pigeons are supposed to fly over, and look for two places to wait in. But we soon get tired of standing still and my brother points me out a house where a couple of sisters live. He whistles at one of them he's had an affair with. She comes down to us; she has big breasts and hairy legs.

"Hey you, see if your sister Adelina will come down too, my brother's here."

The girl goes back to the house and I ask my brother: "Is she pretty, the sister, is she pretty?"

My brother does not give an opinion. "She's fat. She's on."

The pair arrive, and mine is really big and fat, quite all right for an afternoon like that. They try to be difficult at first and say they can't be seen going round with us or they'll make enemies of everyone on the valley, but we tell them not to be silly and take them out to the field and the places where we were waiting for the pigeons to pass. My brother even manages to let off a shot now and again; he is used to taking a girl with him out shooting.

After I've been there a little while with Adelina, another hail of stones hits me in the nape of the neck. I catch sight of the boy with the freckles making off, but don't feel like running after him and just swear at him.

Finally the girls say they have to go to benediction.

"Off with you and don't bother us again," we say.

Then my brother explains to me that they're the two easiest sluts in the valley and are afraid that other young men may see them with us and not go with them any more. "Bitches," I shout at the wind; but at heart I'm sorry that the only girls to go with us are the two easiest sluts in the valley.

In the porch outside the church of San Cosimo and Damiano there's a crowd of people waiting for benediction. They draw back and everyone looks at us askance, even the priest, for the Bagnascos have not been to mass for three generations.

We go on and feel something fall near us. "That boy," we shout, ready to jump round and catch him. But it's only a rotten medlar which has dropped from a branch. On we walk, kicking at the stones.

The House of the Beehives

It is difficult to see from far away and even if someone had already been here once they could not remember the way back; there was a path here at one time, but I made brambles grow over it and wiped out every trace. It's well chosen, this home of mine, lost in this bank of broom, on a single floor that can't be seen from the valley, and covered in a chalky whitewash with windows picked out in red.

There's some land around I could have worked and haven't; a patch for vegetables where snails munch the lettuces is enough for me, and a bit of terraced earth to dig up with a pitch fork and grow potatoes, all purple and budding. I only need to work to feed myself, for I've nothing to share with anyone.

And I don't cut back the brambles, either the ones now clambering over the roof of the house or those already creeping like a slow avalanche over the cultivated ground; I should like them to bury everything, myself included. Then lizards have made their nests in the cracks of the walls, ants have scooped out porous cities under the bricks of the floor, and I look forward every day to seeing if a new crack has opened, and think of the cities of the human race being smothered and swallowed up by weeds.

Above my home are a few strips of rough meadow where I let my goats roam. At dawn dogs sometimes pass by, on the scent of hares; I chase them off with stones. I hate dogs, and their servile fidelity to man, I hate all domestic animals, their pretence of sympathy with human beings just so as to lick the remains off greasy plates. Goats are the only animals I can stand, for they don't expect intimacy or give any.

I don't need chained dogs to guard me. Or even hedges or padlocks, those horrible contraptions of humans. My field is set round with beehives, and a flight of bees is like a thorny hedge which only I can cross. At night the bees sleep in the bean husks, but no man ever comes near my house; they are afraid of me and they are right; not because certain tales which they tell about me are true; lies, I say, just the sort of thing they would tell; but they are right to be afraid of me, I want them to be.

When I go over the crest in the morning, I can see the valley dropping away beneath and the sea high all round me and the world. And I see the houses of the human race perched on the edge of the sea, shipwrecked in their false neighbourliness; I see the tawny chalky city, the glittering of its windows and the smoke of its fires. One day brambles and grass will cover its squares, and the sea will come up and mould the ruins into rocks.

Only the bees are with me, now; they buzz round my hands without stinging me when I take the honey from the hives, and settle on me like a living beard; friendly bees, ancient race without a history. For years I've been living on this bank of broom with goats and bees; once I used to make a mark on the wall at every year that passed; now the brambles choke everything. Why should I live with men and work for them? I loathe their sweaty hands, their savage rites, their dances and churches, their women's acid saliva. But those stories aren't true, believe me; they've always told stories about me, the lying swine.

I don't give anything and I don't owe anything; if it rains at night I cook and eat the big snails slithering down the banks in the morning; the earth in the wood is scattered with soft damp toadstools. The wood gives me everything else I need: sticks and pine-cones to burn, and chestnuts; and I snare hares and thrushes, too, for don't think I love wild animals or have an idyllic adoration of nature—one of man's absurd hypocrisies. I know that in this world we must devour each other and that the law of the strongest holds; I kill just the animals I want to eat, with traps, not with guns, so as not to need dogs or other men to fetch them.

Sometimes I meet men in the wood, if I'm not warned in time by the dull thuds of their axes cutting down trees one by one. I pretend not to see them. On Sundays the poor come to gather fuel in the woods, which they strip like the speckled heads of aloes; the trunks are hauled away on ropes and form rough tracks which gather the rain during storms and provoke landfalls. May everything go to similar ruin in the cities of the human race; may I, as I walk along one day, see the tops of chimneys emerging from the earth, meet parts of streets falling off into ravines, and stumble on strips of railway lines in the middle of the forest.

But you must wonder if I don't ever feel this solitude of mine weighing on me, if some evening, one of those long twilights, one of those first long spring twilights, I've not gone down without any definite idea in my head towards the houses of the human race. I did go, one warm twilight, towards those walls surrounding the gardens below, and climbed down over the medlar trees; but when I heard women laughing and a distant child calling, back I came up here. That was the last time; now I'm up here alone. Well, I get frightened of making a mistake every now and again, as you do. And so, like you, I go on as I was before.

You're afraid of me, of course, and you're right. Not because of that affair, though. That, whether it ever happened or not, was so many years ago it doesn't matter now, anyway.

That woman, that dark woman who came up here to scythe—I had only been up here a short time then and was still full of human emotions—well, I saw her working high on the slope and she hailed me and I didn't reply and passed on. Yes, I was still full of human emotions then, and of an old resentment too; and because of that old resentment—not against her though, as I don't even remember her face—I went up behind her without her hearing me.

Now the tale as people tell it is obviously false, for it was late and there wasn't a soul in the valley and when I put my hands round her throat none heard her. But I would have to tell you my story from the beginning for you to understand.

Ah, well, don't let's mention that evening any more. Here I live, sharing my lettuces with snails which perforate the leaves, and I know all the places where toadstools grow and can tell the good ones from the poisonous; about women and their poisons I don't think any more. Being chaste is nothing but a habit, after all.

She was the last one, that dark woman with the scythe. The sky was full of clouds, I remember, dark clouds scudding along. It must have been under a hurrying sky like that, on slopes cropped by goats, that the first human marriage took place. In contact between human beings there can only, I know, be mutual terror and shame. That's what I wanted; to see the terror and shame, just the terror and shame, in her eyes; that's the only reason I did it to her, believe me.

No one has said a word about it to me, ever; there isn't a word they can say, as the valley was deserted that evening. But every night, when the hills are lost in the dark and I can't follow the meaning of an old book by the light of the lantern, and I sense the town with its human beings and its lights and music down below, I feel the voices of you all accusing me.

But there was no one to see me there in the valley; they say those things because the woman never returned home.

And if dogs passing by always stop to stiff at a certain spot, and bay and scratch the ground with their paws, it's because there's an old moles' lair there, I swear it, just an old moles' lair.

Fear on the Footpath

AT A quarter past nine, just as the moon was getting up, he reached the Colla Bracca meadow; at ten he was already at the cross-roads of the two trees; by half past twelve he'd be at the fountain; he might reach Vendetta's camp by one—ten hours of walking at a normal speed, but six hours at the most for Binda, the courier of the first battalion, the fastest courier in the partisan brigade.

He went hard at it, did Binda, flinging himself headlong down short cuts, never making a mistake at turnings which all looked alike, recognising stones and bushes in the dark. His firm chest never changed the rhythm of his breathing, his legs went like pistons. " Hurry up, Binda! " his comrades would say as they saw him from a distance climbing up towards their camp. They tried to read in his face if the news and orders he was bringing were good or bad; but Binda's face was shut like a fist, a narrow mountaineer's face with hairy lips on a short bony body more like a boy's than a youth's, with muscles like stones.

It was a tough and solitary job, his was, being woken at all hours, sent out even to Serpe's camp or Pelle's, having to march in the dark valleys at night, accompanied only by a French tommy-gun, light as a little wooden rifle, hanging on his shoulder; and when he reached a detachment he had to move on to another or return with the answer; he would wake up the cook and grope around in the cold pots, then leave again with a panful of chestnuts still sticking in his throat. But it was the natural job for him, as

47

he never got lost in the woods and knew all the paths, from having led goats about them or gone there for wood or hay since he was a child; and he never went lame or rubbed the skin off his feet scrambling about the rocks as so many partisans did who'd come up from the towns or the navy.

Glimpses seen as he went along: a chestnut tree with a hollow trunk, blue lichen on a stone, the bare space round a charcoal pit, linked themselves in his mind to his remotest memories—an escaped goat, a pole-cat driven from its lair, the raised skirt of a girl. And now the war in these parts was like a continuation of his normal life; work, play, hunting, all turned into war; the smell of gunpowder at the Loreto bridge, escapes down the bushy slopes, minefields sewn with death.

The war twisted closely round and round in those valleys like a dog trying to bite its tail; partisans elbow to elbow with Bersaglieri and Fascist militia; each side alternating between mountain and valley, making wide turns round the crests so as not to run into each other and find themselves fired on; and always someone killed, either on hill or valley. Binda's village, San Faustino, was down among fields, three groups of houses on each side of the valley. His girl, Regina, hung out sheets from her window on days when there were round ups. Binda's village was a short halt on his way up and down; a sip of milk, a clean vest ready washed by his mother; then off he had to hurry, in case the Fascists suddenly arrived, for there hadn't been enough partisans killed at San Faustino.

All winter it was a game of hide and seek; the Bersaglieri at Baiardo, the Militia at Molini, the Germans at Briga, and in the middle of them the partisans squeezed into two corners of the valley, avoiding the round ups by moving from one to the other during the night. That very night a German column was marching on Briga, had perhaps already reached Carmo, and the Militia were getting ready to reinforce Molini. The partisan detachments were sleeping in stalls around half spent braziers; Binda marched along in the dark woods, with their salvation in his legs, for the order he carried was: " Evacuate the valleys at once. Entire battalion and heavy machine guns to be on Mount Pellegrino by dawn."

Binda felt anxiety fluttering in his lungs like bats' wings; he longed to grasp the slope two miles away, pull himself up it, whisper the order like a breath of wind into the grass and hear it flowing off through his moustache and nostrils, till it reached Vendetta, Serpe, Gueriglia; then scoop himself out a hole in the chestnut leaves and bury himself in there, he and Regina, first taking out the cones that might prick Regina's legs; but the more leaves he scooped out the more cones he found—it was impossible to make a place for Regina's legs there, her big soft legs with their smooth thin skin.

The dry leaves and the chestnut cones rustled, almost gurgled, under Binda's feet; the squirrels with their round glittering eyes ran to hide at the tops of the trees. " Be quick, Binda!" the commander, Fegato, had said to him when giving him the message. Sleep rose from the heart of the night, there was a velvety feel on the inside of his eyelids; Binda would have liked to lose the path, plunge into a sea of dry leaves and swim in them until they submerged him. " Be quick, Binda!"

He was now walking on a narrow path along the upper slopes of the Tumena valley, which was still covered with ice. It was the widest valley in the area, and had high sides wide apart; the one opposite him was glimmering in the dark, the one on which he was walking had bare slopes scattered with an occasional bush from which, in daytime, rose fluttering groups of partridges. Binda felt he saw a distant light, down in lower Tumena, moving ahead of him. It zig-zagged every now and again as if going round a curve, vanished, and reappeared a little farther on in an unexpected part. Who on earth could it be at that hour? Sometimes it seemed to Binda that the light was much farther away, on the other side of the valley, sometimes that it had stopped, and sometimes that it was behind him. Who could be carrying so many different lights along all the paths of lower Tumena, perhaps in front of him too, in higher Tumena, winking on and off like that? The Germans!

Following on Binda's tracks was an animal roused from deep back in his childhood; it was coming after him, would soon catch him up; the animal of fear. Those lights were the Germans searching Tumena, bush by bush, in battalions. Impossible, Binda knew that, although it would be almost pleasant to believe it, to abandon himself to the blandishments of that animal from childhood which was following him so close. Time was drumming, gulping in Binda's throat. Perhaps it was too late now to arrive before the Germans and save his comrades. Already Binda could see Vendetta's hut at Castagna burnt out, the bleeding bodies of his comrades, the heads of some of them hanging by their long hair on branches of larch trees. "Be quick, Binda!"

He was amazed at where he was, he seemed to have gone such a little way in such a long time; perhaps he had slowed down or even stopped without realising it. He did not change his pace, however; he knew well that it was always regular and sure, that he mustn't trust that animal which came to visit him on these night missions, wetting his temples with its invisible fingers slimy with saliva. He was a healthy lad, Binda, with good nerves, cool in every eventuality; and he kept intact all his power to act even though he was carrying that animal around with him like a monkey tethered to his neck.

The surface of the Colla Bracca meadow looked soft in the moonlight. "Mines!" thought Binda. There were no mines up there, Binda knew that; they were a long way off, on the other slope of the mountain. But Binda now began thinking that the mines might have moved underground from one part of the mountain to the other, following his steps like enormous underground spiders. The earth above mines produces strange funguses, disastrous to knock over; everything would go up in a second, but each second would become as long as a century and the world would have stopped as if by magic.

Now Binda was going down through the wood. Drowsiness and darkness drew gloomy masks on the tree trunks and bushes. There were Germans all round. They must have seen him pass the Colla Bracca meadow in the moonlight, they were following him, waiting for him at the entrance to the wood. An owl hooted nearby: it was a whistle, a signal for the Germans to close in round him. There, another whistle, he was surrounded! An animal moved at the back of a bush of heather; perhaps it was a hare, perhaps a fox, perhaps a German lying in the thickets keeping him covered. There was a German in every thicket, a German perched on the top of every tree, with the squirrels. The stones were pullulating with helmets, rifles were sprouting among the branches, the roots of the trees ended in human feet. Binda was walking between a double row of hidden Germans, who were looking at him with glistening eyes from between the leaves; the farther he walked the deeper he got in among them. At the third, the fourth, the sixth hoot of the owl all the Germans would jump to their feet round him, their guns pointed, their chests crossed by sten-gun straps.

One called Gund, in the middle of them, with a terrible white smile under his helmet, would stretch out huge hands to seize him. Binda was afraid to turn round in case he saw Gund looming above his shoulders, sten-gun at the ready, hands open in the air. Or perhaps Gund would appear on the path ahead, pointing a finger at him, or come up and begin walking silently along beside him.

Suddenly he thought he had missed the way; and yet he recognised the path, the stones, the trees, the smell of musk. But they were stones, trees, musk from another place far away, from a thousand different far away places. After these stone steps there should be a short drop, not a bramble bush. After that slope a bush of broom, not of holly; the side of the path should be dry, not full of water and frogs. The frogs were in another valley, they were near the Germans; at the turn of the path there was a German ambush waiting and he'd suddenly fall into their hands, find himself facing the big German called Gund who is deep down in all of us, and who opens his enormous hands above us all, yet never succeeds in catching us.

To drive away Gund he must think of Regina, scoop a niche for Regina in the snow; but the snow is hard and frozen—Regina can't sit on it in her thin dress; nor can she sit under the pines— there are endless layers of pine needles; the earth underneath is all ant heaps, and Gund is already above, lowering his hands on to their heads and throats, lowering still . . . he gave a shriek. No, he must think of Regina, the girl who is in all of us and for whom we all want to scoop a niche deep in the woods—the girl with big hips and dressed only in hair which falls down over her shoulders.

But the pursuit between Binda and Gund is nearing its end; Vendetta's camp is now only fifteen, twenty minutes away. Binda's thoughts run ahead; but his feet go on placing themselves regularly one in front of the other so as not to lose breath. When he reaches his comrades his fear will have vanished, cancelled even from the bottom of his memory as something impossible. He must think of waking up Vendetta and Sciabola, the commissar, to explain Fegato's order to them; then he'd set off again for Serpe's camp.

But would he ever reach the hut? Wasn't he tied by a wire which dragged him farther away the nearer he got? And as he arrived wouldn't he hear *ausch ausch* from Germans sitting round the fire eating up the remaining chestnuts? Binda imagined himself arriving at the hut to find it half burnt out and deserted. He went inside: empty. But in a corner, huge, sitting on his haunches, with his helmet touching the ceiling, was Gund, with his eyes round and glistening like the squirrels' and his white toothy smile between damp lips. Gund would make a sign to him: " Sit down." And Binda would sit down.

There, a hundred yards off, a light! It was them! Which of them? He longed to turn back, to flee, as if all the danger was up there in the hut. But he went on walking quickly along, his face hard and closed like a fist. Now the fire suddenly seemed to be getting too near; was it moving to meet him? Now to be getting farther off; was it running away? But it was motionless, a camp-fire which had not yet gone out, Binda knew that.

"Who goes there?" He did not quiver an eyelash. "Binda," he said.

Sentry: "I'm Civetta. Any news, Binda?"

"Is Vendetta asleep?"

Now he was inside the hut, with sleeping comrades breathing all round him. Comrades, of course; who could ever have thought they'd be anything else?

"Germans down at Briga, Fascists up at Molini. Evacuate. By dawn you've all to be up on the crest of Mount Pellegrino with the heavies."

Vendetta was scarcely awake and fluttering his eyelids. "God," he said. Then he got up, clapped his hands. "Wake up, everyone, we've got to go out and fight."

Binda was now sucking at a can of boiled chestnuts, spitting out the bits of skin sticking to them. The men divided up into shifts for carrying the ammunition and the tripod of the heavy. He set off. "I'm going on to Serpe's," he said. "Be quick, Binda!" exclaimed his comrades.

Hunger at Bévera

THE FRONT had stopped there, as it had in '40, except that this time the war did not end and there seemed no chance of things moving. People did not want to do as they had in '40, load a few rags and chickens on to a cart, and set off with a mule in front and a goat behind. When they got back in '40 they had found all their drawers overturned on the floor and human excrement in the cooking pots; for Italians, when soldiers, don't bother if the damage they do is to friends or enemies. So people stayed on, with the French shells hitting their houses day and night and the German shells whistling over their heads.

"One day or other, when they really decide to advance," people said, and had to go on repeating this to each other from September to April, "they'll put their backs into it, those blessed Allies will."

The valley of Bévera was full of people, peasants and also refugees from Ventimiglia, and they had nothing to eat; there were no reserves of food, and flour had to be fetched from the town. And the road into the town was under shell fire night and day.

By now they were living more in holes than in houses; and one day the men of the village collected in a cave to decide what to do.

"What we'll have to do," said the man from the Committee

54

of Liberation, " is take it in turns to go down to Ventimiglia and fetch bread."

" Fine," said another. " So one by one we'll all be blown to bits on the way."

" Or if not the Germans will get us one by one and off we'll go to Germany," said a third.

And another asked: " What about an animal to transport the stuff? Will anyone offer theirs? No one'll risk it who still has one. Obviously whoever gets through won't come back, nor will animals or bread."

The animals had already been requisitioned and anyone who'd saved his kept it hidden.

" Well," said the man from the Committee. " If we don't get bread here how are we going to live? Is there anyone who feels like taking a mule down to Ventimiglia? I'm wanted by the Fascists down there or I'd go myself."

He looked around; the men were sitting on the ground of the cave with expressionless eyes, scooping at the tufa with their fingers.

Then old Bisma, who'd been down at the end, looking round with his mouth open not understanding anything, got up and went out of the cave. The others thought he wanted to urinate as he was old and needed to every now and again.

" Careful, Bisma," they shouted after him. " Do it under cover."

But he did not turn round.

" As far as he's concerned they mightn't be shelling at all," someone said.. " He's deaf and doesn't notice."

Bisma was more than eighty and his back seemed permanently bent under a load of faggots—all the faggots he had hauled throughout his life from woods to stalls. They called him Bisma because of his moustaches which had once, they said, looked like Bismarck's; now they were a pair of scraggy white tufts which seemed about to fall off at any moment, like all the other parts of his body.

But nothing fell off, though, and Bisma dragged himself along, his head swaying, with the expressionless and rather mistrusting look that deaf people have.

He reappeared at the mouth of the cave.

" Iiii ! " he was calling.

Then the others saw that he was dragging his mule behind him, and that he'd put on its pack-saddle. Bisma's mule seemed older than its master; its neck was flat as a board and hung to the ground, and its movements were cautious, as if the jutting bones were about to break through the skin and appear through the sores, black with flies.

" Where're you taking the mule to, Bisma ? " they asked.

He swayed his head from side to side, with his mouth open. He couldn't hear.

" The sacks," he said. " Give me them."

" Hey," they exclaimed. " How far d'you think you're going to get, you and that old bag of bones ? "

" How many kilos ? " he asked. " Eh ! How many kilos ? "

They gave him the sacks, they explained the number of kilos on their fingers and off he set. At every whistle of a shell the men peered from the threshold of the cave at the road and at that bent figure drawing farther away; both the mule and the man riding on the pack-saddle seemed to be swaying and looking as if they were about to fall down at any minute. The shells were falling ahead of them on the track, raising a thick dust, pitting the track in front of the mule's cautious steps; and when they fell behind Bisma did not even turn round. At every shell fired, at every whistle, the men held their breath. " This one'll get him," they said. Suddenly he vanished altogether, wrapped in dust. The men were silent; now, when the dust settled they would see a bare road, without even a trace of him. Instead they both reappeared like ghosts, the man and the mule, and went on hobbling slowly along. Then they got to the last turn in the road and moved out of sight. "He won't make it," said the men, and turned their backs.

But Bisma went on riding along the stony road. The old mule went on putting down its hoofs uncertainly on the surface pitted with flints and new holes; its skin was stretched tight with the burning of the sores under its pack-saddle. The explosions made no impression on it; it had suffered so much in its life that nothing could make any impression on it any more. It was walking along with its muzzle bent down, and its eyes, limited by the black blinkers, were noticing all sorts of things; snails, broken by the shelling, spilling an iridescent slime on the stones: ant-hills ripped open and the black and white ants hurrying hither and thither with eggs; torn-up grasses showing strange hairy roots like trees.

And the man riding on the pack-saddle was trying to keep himself upright on the thin haunches, while all his poor bones were starting in their sockets at the roughness of the road. But he had lived his life with mules and his ideas were as few and as resigned as theirs; it had always been long and tiring to find his bread, bread for himself and bread for others, and now bread for the whole of Bévera. The world, this silent world which surrounded him, seemed to be trying to speak to him too, with confused boomings which reached even his sleeping eardrums, and strange disturbances of the earth. He could see banks crumbling, clouds rising from the fields, stones flying, and red flashes appearing and disappearing on the hills; the world was trying to change its old face and show its underpart of earth and roots. And the silence, the terrible silence of his old age, was ruffled by those distant sounds.

The road at the mule's feet sent out huge sparks, its nostrils and throat were filled with earth, a hail of splintered stones hit the man and the mule from the side while the branches of a big olive tree whirled in the air above his head; and yet he wouldn't fall unless the mule fell. And the mule held on, its hoofs rooted in the torn-up earth, its knees just not giving way.

In the evening, up at Bévera someone shouted: " Look! It's Bisma coming back! He's made it! "

Then the men and women and children came out of the houses and caves and saw the mule at the last turn of the road, coming ahead more bent than ever under the weight of sacks, and Bisma behind, on foot, hanging on to its tail so that they couldn't tell if he was pushing or being pulled.

Bisma had a great welcome from the people of the valley when he got in with the bread. It was distributed in the big cave; the inhabitants passed through one by one and the man from the Committee handed out a loaf a head. Near him stood Bisma munching his loaf with his few teeth and looking round at everyone.

And Bisma went to Ventimiglia the next day too. His mule was the only animal the Germans were sure not to want. And he went on going down every day to fetch bread, and every day he passed unhurt through the shells; he must have made a deal with the devil, they said.

Then the Germans evacuated the left bank of the Bévera river, blew up two bridges and a piece of road and laid down mines. The inhabitants were given forty-eight hours to leave the village and the area. They left the village but not the area; back they went into their holes. But now they were isolated, caught between two fronts and with no way of getting supplies. It meant starvation.

When they heard the village had been evacuated, the Black Brigade came up. They were singing. One of them was carrying a tin of paint and a brush. On the walls he wrote: *They shall not pass. We go straight ahead. The Axis does not give way.*

Meanwhile the others were wandering round the streets, with sten-guns on their shoulders, glancing at the houses. Then they began breaking in a door or two with their shoulders. At that moment Bisma appeared on his mule. He appeared at the top of a road on a slope, and came down between two rows of houses.

"Hey, where are you going?" said the men of the Black Brigade.

The old man did not seem to see them, the mule went on putting one wobbly leg in front of the other.

"Hey, we're talking to you!" The haggard impassive old man, perched on that skeleton of a mule, seemed a ghost issued from the stones of the uninhabited and half-ruined village.

"He's deaf," they said.

The old man looked at them, one by one. The Black Brigade men went down a side alley. They reached a little square where the only sounds were water trickling in the fountain and distant guns.

"I know there's stuff in that house," said one of the Black Brigade, pointing. He was only a boy, with a red blotch under his eye. The echo among the houses of the empty square repeated his words one by one. The boy made a nervous gesture. The one with the brush wrote on a ruined wall: *Honour is Struggle*. A window that had been left open was banging and making more noise than the guns.

"Wait," said the boy with the red blotch to two others who were pushing at a door. He put the mouth of his sten-gun against the lock and fired a burst. The lock, all burnt out, gave way. At that moment Bisma reappeared again from the opposite direction to the one where they'd left him. He seemed to be promenading up and down the village on that ruin of a mule.

"Wait till he's passed," said one of the Black Brigade, and they stood in front of the door looking indifferent.

Rome or Death, wrote the man with the brush.

Very slowly, the mule crossed the square; every step seemed to be its last. The man riding it appeared to be on the point of falling asleep.

"Go away," shouted the boy with the blotch. "The village is evacuated."

Bisma did not turn round; he seemed intent on piloting his mule across that empty square.

"If we see you again," went on the same boy, "we'll shoot." *We shall win*, wrote the man with the brush.

Now only Bisma's decrepit back could be seen above the black legs of the mule, which seemed almost halted.

"Let's go down there," decided the Black Brigade men and they turned under an arch.

"Hey. No time to lose. Let's begin with this house." They opened it up and the boy with the blotch entered first. The house was empty, with nothing in it but echoes. They wandered round the rooms and came out again.

"I'd like to set fire to the whole village, I would," said the boy with the blotch.

We shall go straight ahead, wrote the other man.

At the end of the little alley reappeared Bisma. He advanced towards them.

"Don't," said the Black Brigade men to the boy with the blotch, who was taking aim.

Duce, wrote the other man.

But the boy with the blotch had let off a burst. They were mown down together, the man and the mule, but still remained on foot. It seemed as if the mule had fallen on its four hoofs and still black spindly legs, all in one piece. The Black Brigade stood looking on; the boy with the blotch had loosened the sten-gun on its belt and was picking his teeth. Then they bowed together, man and mule; they seemed to take another step, instead of which down they fell on top of each other.

That night the people of the village came to take them away. Bisma they buried; the mule they cooked and ate. It was tough meat, but they were hungry.

Going to Headquarters

IT WAS a sparse wood, almost destroyed by fire, grey with charred tree trunks amid the dry reddish needles of the pines. Two men, one armed, the other unarmed, were zig-zagging down between the trees.

"To headquarters," the armed man was saying. "To headquarters, that's where we're going. Half an hour's walk at the most."

"And then?"

"Then what?"

"Then will they let me go?" said the unarmed man. He was listening to every syllable of every reply as if searching for a false note.

"Yes, they'll let you go," said the armed man. "I hand them the papers from battalion, they enter them on their list, then you can go home."

The unarmed man shook his head and looked pessimistic.

"Oh, they take a long time, these things do. I know . . ." he said, perhaps just to hear the other man repeat:

"They'll let you go at once, I tell you."

"I was hoping," he went on, "I was hoping to be home this afternoon. Ah, well, patience."

"You'll make it, I tell you," replied the armed man. "Just a few questions, and they'll let you go. They've got to cross off your name from the list of spies."

" Have you got a list of spies? "

" Of course we have. We know 'em all, the spies. And we get 'em, one by one."

" And my name's on it? "

" Yes, your name too. They must cross it off properly now, or you risk being taken again."

" Then I really should go there myself, so's to explain the whole thing to them."

" We're going there now. They have to look into it properly to check."

" But by now," said the unarmed man, " by now you all know I'm on your side and have never been a spy."

" Just so. We know all about it now. You needn't worry now."

The unarmed man nodded and looked around. They were in a big clearing, with mangy pines and larches killed by fire and draped with fallen branches. They had left, refound and lost the path again, and were walking apparently at random among the scattered pines through the wood. The unarmed man did not know this part. Evening was creeping up in thin layers of mist. Down below the woods were lost in the dark. It worried him, their leaving the path; as the other seemed to be walking at random. He tried bearing towards the right, hoping to find the path again: the other also bore to the right, apparently at random. Then the unarmed man turned wherever the walking was easier, with the armed man following him.

He decided to ask: " But where's the headquarters? "

" We're going towards it," replied the armed man. " You'll soon see it now."

" But what place, what part is it, more or less? "

" Well," he replied, " one can't say headquarters is in any place or part. Headquarters is wherever it is. You understand? "

He understood; he was a person who understood things, the unarmed man was. But he asked: " Isn't there a path to it? "

The other replied: "A path? You understand. A path always goes somewhere. One doesn't get to headquarters by paths. You understand."

The unarmed man understood, he was a person who understood things, an astute man.

He asked: "D'you often go to headquarters?"

"Often," said the armed man. "Yes, often."

He had a sad face, with a vacant look. Apparently he didn't know those parts very well. Every now and again he seemed lost, and yet went walking on as if it did not matter.

"And why have they told you to take me along to-day?" asked the unarmed man, scrutinising him.

"That's my job, to take you along," he replied. "I'm the one who takes people along to headquarters."

"You're their courier, are you?"

"That's right," said the armed man. "Their courier."

"A strange courier"—thought the unarmed man—"who doesn't know the way. But"—he thought—"to-day he doesn't want to go by the paths in case I realise where the headquarters is, for they don't trust me. A bad sign, their not trusting me yet," the unarmed man couldn't help thinking. But though it was a bad sign, it did mean that they really were bringing him to headquarters and intended to let him go free. Another bad sign, apart from this, was that the wood was getting thicker and thicker. Then there was the silence and this gloomy armed man.

"Did you take the Secretary along to headquarters too? And the brothers from the mill? And the schoolmistress?" He asked this question all in one breath, without stopping to think, for it was the decisive question, the question which meant everything; the Secretary of the Commune, the brothers from the mill, the schoolmistress, were all people who had been taken off and never returned, of whom nothing more had ever been heard again.

"The Secretary was a Fascist," said the armed man. "The

brothers from the mill were in the Militia, the schoolmistress worked with the Fascists."

"I only just wondered, as they'd never come back."

"What I mean is," insisted the armed man, "they were what they were. You're what you are. There's no comparison."

"Of course," said the other. "There's no comparison. I only asked what had happened to them just out of curiosity."

He felt sure of himself, the unarmed man did, enormously sure of himself. He was the astutest man in the village, it was difficult to do him down. The others, the Secretary and the schoolmistress, had not come back; he would come back. "I big *kamarad*," he would say to the German sergeant. "Partisan not *kaput* me. I *kaput* all partisans." Perhaps the sergeant might laugh.

But the burnt trees seemed interminable and ambiguous and his thoughts were surrounded by darkness and the unknown, like the bare spaces in the middle of this wood.

"I don't know about the Secretary and the others. I'm the courier."

"They'll know at headquarters though?" insisted the unarmed man.

"Yes. Ask them at headquarters. They'll know there."

Dusk was falling. He had to walk carefully in the undergrowth, taking care where his feet went in case they slipped on rocks hidden under the thick scrub; and taking care where his thoughts went too, as they followed each other in growing disquiet, in case they suddenly plunged headlong into panic.

Surely if they'd thought him a spy they would never have let him go through the woods like this, alone with this man who didn't seem to be taking any notice of him at all; he could have escaped from him any time he wanted. Suppose he tried to escape now, what would he do, the other man?

As he wound down among the trees the unarmed man began to draw a little way off, to bear to the left when the other bore to the right. But the armed man went on walking almost, it seemed, without taking any notice of him; down through the sparse woods they went, now some distance from each other. Sometimes they even lost sight of each other, hidden by trunks and shrubs, then suddenly the unarmed man would turn round and see the other above him.

" If they let me free for a moment, this time they won't get me again," the unarmed man had thought till then. But now he surprised himself thinking: " If I manage to escape, then this time . . ." And already in his mind he saw Germans, columns of Germans, Germans in lorries and armoured cars, a sight that meant death for the others and safety for him who was an astute man, a man no one could get the better of.

Now they were out of the glades and undergrowth and entering thick green woods, untouched by fire; the ground was covered with dry pine needles. The armed man had remained behind, perhaps he had taken another route. Then, very cautiously, his tongue between his teeth, the unarmed man hurried his pace, pushing deeper into the thick woods, flinging himself down slopes, among the pine trees. He was escaping, he suddenly realised. He had a moment of panic then; but he realised also that he'd got too far away now and that the other must have noticed he was trying to escape and was sure to be following him. The only thing to do was go on running, as things might be ugly if he came under the other's range again after trying to escape.

He turned at the sound of a footstep above him; a few yards away was the armed man coming towards him with his calm, indifferent pace. His gun was in his hand. He said: " There must be a short cut this way," and made a sign for the other to go ahead of him.

Everything then returned as it was before: an ambiguous world, where things might go completely wrong or completely right; the wood thickening instead of thinning out, this man who'd almost let him escape without a word.

He asked: " Does it go on for ever, though, this wood? "

"Just round the hillside and there we are," said the other. "Bear up, you'll be home by to-night."

"Are they sure to let me go, just like that? I mean, won't they keep me there as a hostage, for instance?"

"We aren't Germans, we don't take hostages. At the most they might take your boots for hostages, as we're all nearly barefoot."

The man began to grumble as if his boots were the one thing he was frightened of losing, but at heart he was pleased; every detail of his future, good or bad, helped to restore a slight feeling of confidence.

"Well," said the armed man. "As you hold by your boots so much let's do this; you put mine on until we get to headquarters, and as mine are all to pieces they won't take them off you. I'll put on yours and when I come back with you hand them over again."

Even a child would have realised this was all just a trick. The armed man wanted his boots, all right the unarmed man would give him whatever he wanted, he was a man who understood, and pleased at getting off so cheaply. "I great *kamarad*," he'd say to the German sergeant. "I give them boots and they let me go." Perhaps the sergeant would let him have a pair of knee-boots like the ones German soldiers wore.

"Then you don't hold anyone hostage? Not even the Secretary and the others?"

"The Secretary had three of our comrades taken; the brothers from the mill went on round ups with the Militia, the school-mistress went to bed with the men of the 10th Flotilla."[1]

The unarmed man halted. He said: "You don't by any chance think I'm a spy too? You haven't by any chance brought me here to kill me?" And he bared a few teeth as if in a smile.

"If we thought you a spy," said the armed man, "I wouldn't do this." He snapped back the safety catch of the gun. "And

[1] 10th Motor Torpedo-boat Flotilla (Decima Mas); Fascist Marines.

this," he put it to his shoulder and made a motion as if about to fire at him.

"There," thought the spy. "He's not firing."

But the other never lowered his gun; he pressed the trigger instead.

"In salvoes, it fires in salvoes," the spy had just time to think. And when he felt the bullets hitting him like fiery fists that never stopped, the thought still crossed his mind: "He thinks he's killed me, but I'm alive."

He fell face downwards and the last shot caught him with a vision of stockinged feet and his boots being pulled off.

So he remained, a corpse in the depth of the wood, with his mouth full of pine-needles. Two hours later he was already black with ants.

The Crow Comes Last

THE CURRENT was a network of light transparent ripples with the water flowing in the middle. Every now and again silver wings seemed to flutter on the surface, a trout's back glittering before it zig-zagged down.

" It's full of trout," said one of the men.

" If we throw a grenade in they'll all come to the surface with their bellies in the air," said the other; he took a grenade from his belt and began to unscrew the cap.

Then a boy who was looking on came forward, a mountaineer with an apple face. " Give me it," he said and took the rifle from one of the men. " What does he want?" said the man and tried to take the rifle away. But the boy was aiming the gun at the water as if looking for a target. " If you fire into the water you'll frighten the fish, that's all," the man tried to say, but he didn't even finish. A trout had surfaced with a flash, and the boy had fired a shot at it as if expecting it at that very spot. And the trout was now floating with its white belly in the air. " O . . . o . . . oh! " said the men. The boy reloaded the gun and swung it round; the air was bright and tight; the pine-needles on the other bank and the ripples on the current showed up clearly. Something darted to the surface; another trout. He fired; it was floating, dead. The men looked at the trout and then at him. " He's a good shot, this lad," they said.

The boy swung the muzzle of the gun round again. It was

strange, thinking it over, to be so surrounded by air, separated from other things by yards of air. When he aimed the gun, on the other hand, the air was a straight invisible line drawn tight from the mouth of the rifle to the target, to the hawk flying up there in the sky with wings which did not seem to move. When he pressed the trigger the air was still empty and transparent as before, but up there at the other end of the line the hawk was folding its wings and dropping like a stone. From the open bolt floated a good smell of gunpowder.

They gave him some more cartridges when he asked for them. Lots of men were looking on now from the bank behind him. "Why," he thought, "could he see the pine-cones at the tops of the trees on the other bank and not touch them? Why was there this empty distance between things and himself? Why were the pine-cones which seemed part of him, inside his eyes, so far away instead?" Surely it was an illusion when he aimed the gun into the empty distance and touched the trigger and at the same second a pine-cone dropped in smithereens? The sense of emptiness felt like a caress—emptiness inside the rifle barrel continuing through the air and filling out when he shot; the pine-cone up there, a squirrel, a white stone, a butterfly. "He never misses once, this lad," said the men, and none of them felt like laughing.

"You come with us," said the commander. "If you give me a rifle," replied the boy. "Well, of course." So he went.

He left with two cheeses and a haversack full of apples. The village was a blotch of slate, straw and cow's dung at the bottom of the valley. It was fine going off because there were new things to be seen at every turn, trees with cones, birds flying from branches, lichen on stones, all in range of those false distances, the distances that could be filled by a shot swallowing the air in between. He must not fire, though, they told him; these were parts which had to be passed in silence and the cartridges were needed for the war. But at a certain point a hare, frightened by their steps, ran across the path amid waves and shouts from the men. Just as it was

vanishing into the thickets a bullet from the boy stopped it.
" Good shot," even the commander said, " but we're not out
hunting here. You mustn't fire again even if you see a pheasant."
Not an hour passed before more shots rang out from the file of
men. " That boy again! " cried the commander furiously and went
up to him. The boy was laughing all over his pink and white
apple face. " Partridges," he said, showing them. " They got up
from a thicket." " Partridges, or grasshoppers, I told you, Give
me that rifle. And if you make me angry again, back you go home."
The boy grumbled a bit; it wasn't much fun walking along
unarmed, but if he stayed with them there was always a chance
of getting the rifle back.

That night they slept in a shepherd's hut. The boy woke up
as the first light was showing in the sky, while the others were
asleep. He took their best rifle, filled his haversack with cartridges
and off he went. The early morning air was mild and bright. Not
far from the hut was a mulberry tree. It was the time when the
jays arrived. There was one; he fired, ran to fetch it and put it
in his haversack. Without moving from the spot where he'd
taken it up he tried another target; a squirrel! Terrified by the
shot, it was running to hide at the top of a chestnut tree. It was
dead now, a big squirrel with a grey tail, which shed tufts of hair
when touched. From under the chestnut tree he saw a toadstool,
red with white spots, poisonous, in a meadow lower down. He
pulverised it with a shot, then went to see if he had really hit it.
It was a lovely game going like this from one target to another;
perhaps he could go round the world doing it. He saw a big
snail on a stone, aimed at its shell and when he got to the place
only found the splintered stone, and a little iridescent slime. So
he gradually got farther and farther away from the hut, down
among unknown fields.

From the stone he saw a lizard on a wall, from the wall a puddle
and a frog, from the puddle a signpost on the road with a zig-zag
on it and below it . . . below it were men in uniform coming up

with arms at the ready. When they saw that boy with a rifle smiling all over his pink and white apple face, they shouted and aimed their guns at him. But the boy had already picked out some gilt buttons on one of their chests and fired at a button. He heard the men's shout and the bullets whistling singly or in bursts over his head; but he was now lying stretched on the ground behind a heap of stones on the edge of the road, under cover. It was a long heap, and he could move about, peep over in some unexpected part, see the gleam on the barrels of the soldiers' weapons, the grey and glittering parts on their uniforms, shoot at a stripe, a badge. Then back he'd drop to the ground and slide quickly over to another side to fire. After a bit he heard bursts from behind him firing over his head and hitting the soldiers; these were his comrades coming to reinforce him with machine-guns. " If that boy hadn't woken us with his shots . . ." they were saying.

Covered by his comrades' fire, the boy could take better aim. Suddenly a bullet grazed one of his cheeks. He turned; a soldier had reached the road above him. He flung himself into a hole under cover, but had fired meanwhile and hit not the soldier but the rifle, by the bolt. He heard the soldier trying to reload, then fling the gun on the ground. The boy looked out then and fired at the soldier, who'd taken to his heels; the bullet tore off a shoulder-strap.

He followed. Every now and again the soldier vanished in the wood, then reappeared. The boy nipped off the top of his helmet, then a strap on his belt. Meanwhile they had reached a remote valley where the sound of battle could no longer be heard. Suddenly the soldier found there were no more woods in front of him, only a glade, with thick bushy slopes. The boy was just coming out of the wood now; in the middle of the glade was a big rock; the soldier just had time to crouch down behind it, with his head between his knees. There for the moment he felt safe; he had some hand grenades with him and the boy could get no nearer, but only keep the rock covered in case the soldier tried to escape. If only, thought the soldier, he could reach the bushes with a rush and slide down the thickly covered slope. But that bare space had to be crossed—how long would the boy stay there? And would he never lower that gun?

The soldier decided to make a test; he put his helmet on the point of his bayonet and hoisted it slightly above the rock. A shot rang out and the helmet rolled to the ground, pierced through.

The soldier did not lose heart; it was obviously easy to aim at the edges of the rock, but if he moved quickly it should be impossible to hit him. At that moment a bird winged quickly across the sky; a pigeon perhaps. A shot and it fell. The soldier dried the sweat on his neck. Another bird passed, a thrush; that fell too. The soldier swallowed saliva. This must be a place of passage; birds went on flying overhead, all of them different, and the boy went on shooting and bringing them down. An idea came to the soldier: " If he is watching the birds he won't be watching me so much. The second he fires I'll run for it." But perhaps it would be better to make a test first. He took up the helmet again and put it back on the point of his bayonet, ready. Two birds passed together, snipe. The soldier was sorry to waste such a good opportunity for the test, but he did not dare risk it yet. The boy fired at one of the snipe, then the soldier pushed up the helmet, heard the shot and saw the helmet whirl in the air.

Now the soldier felt a taste of lead in his mouth; he scarcely noticed the other bird falling at a new shot. He must not hurry things, anyway; he was safe behind that rock, with his grenades. And why not try and get him with a grenade, while staying under cover? He stretched back on the ground, drew his arm out behind him, taking care not to show himself, gathered up all his strength and threw the grenade. A good effort; it would have gone a long way; but in the middle of its flight a shot exploded it in mid-air. The soldier flung himself on the ground to avoid the shrapnel.

When he raised his head the crow had come. It was swinging

slowly round in the sky above him. "Was it a crow," he thought? Now the boy would be certain to shoot it down. But the shot seemed to be a long time in coming. Perhaps the crow was flying too high? And yet he had hit other birds flying higher and faster. Finally there was a shot; now the crow would fall, but no, it went on flying round in slow impassive turns. A pine-cone fell, though, from a tree nearby. Was he beginning to shoot at pine-cones now? One by one other pine-cones were hit and fell with little thuds. At every shot the soldier looked at the crow; was he falling? No, the black bird was making lower and lower turns above him. Surely it was impossible the boy hadn't seen it? Perhaps the crow did not exist? Perhaps it was a hallucination of his? Perhaps when one is about to die one sees every kind of bird pass; when one sees the crow it means one's time has come. He must warn the boy, who was still going on firing at the pine-cones. So the soldier got to his feet and pointed at the black bird. " There's a crow!" he shouted in his own language. The bullet hit him in the middle of an eagle with spread wings embroidered on his tunic.

Slowly the crow came circling down.

One of the Three is Still Alive

THREE NAKED men were sitting on a stone. Around them were standing all the men of the village, with a bearded old man facing them.

". . . and they were the highest flames I've ever seen in the mountains," the old man with the beard was saying. " And I said to myself: how can a village burn so high?

" And the smell of smoke was unbearable and I said to myself: how can smoke from our village stink like that?"

The tallest of the three naked men, who was hugging his shoulders because there was a slight wind, gave the oldest a dig in the ribs to get him to explain; he still wanted to understand and the other was the only one who knew a little of the language. But the oldest of the three did not raise his head from between his hands, and now and again a quiver passed along the vertebrae on his bent back. The fat man was no longer to be counted on; the womanly fat on his body was trembling all over, his eyes were like window-panes streaked by rain.

" And then they told me that the flames burning our houses came from our own grain, and the stink was from our sons being burnt alive; Tancin's son, Gé's son, the son of the customs guard . . ."

" My son Bastian! " shouted a man with haunted eyes. He was the only one who interrupted, every now and again. The others

74

were standing there silent and serious, with their hands on their rifles.

The third naked man was not of exactly the same nationality as the others; he came from a part where villages and children had been burnt at one time. So he knew what people think about those who burn and kill and should have felt less hopeful than the others. Instead of which there was something, an anguished uncertainty that prevented him resigning himself.

"Now we've only caught these three men," said the old man with the beard.

"Only three!" shouted the haunted-looking man, but the others were still silent.

"Maybe among them, too, there are some who aren't really bad, who obey orders against their will, maybe these three are that sort . . ."

The haunted-looking man glared at the old man.

"Explain," whispered the tallest of the three naked men to the oldest. But the other's whole life now seemed to be running away down the vertebrae on his spine.

"When children have been killed and houses burnt one can't make any distinction between those who're bad and not bad. And we're sure of being in the right by condemning these three to death."

"Death," thought the tallest of the three naked men. "I heard that word. What does it mean—'Death'?"

But the oldest of them took no notice of him and the fattest now seemed to be muttering prayers. Suddenly the fattest had remembered he was a Catholic. He had been the only Catholic in the company and his comrades had often made fun of him. "I'm a Catholic," he began muttering in his own language. It was not clear if he was begging for salvation on earth or in heaven.

"I say that before killing them we should . . ." exclaimed the haunted-looking man, but the others had got to their feet and were not listening to him.

" To the Witch's Hole," said one with black moustaches. " So there won't be any graves to dig."

They made the three get up. The fattest put his hands over his front. Nothing made them feel more under accusation than being naked.

They led them up along the rocky path, with rifles in their backs. The Witch's Hole was the opening of a vertical cave, a hole which dropped right down into the belly of the mountain, down, down, no one knew where. The three naked men were led up to the edge and the armed peasants lined up in front of them; then the oldest of them began screaming. He screamed out despairing phrases, perhaps in his own dialect; the other two did not understand him; he was the father of a family, the oldest of them was, but he was also the worst and his screams had the effect of making the other two feel annoyed with him and calmer in the face of death. The tall one, though, still felt that strange disquiet, as if he were not quite certain of something. The Catholic was holding his joined hands low; it was not clear if this was to pray, or to hide his front.

Hearing the oldest of them screaming made the armed peasants lose their calm; they wanted to have done with the business as soon as possible, and began to fire scattered shots without waiting for an order. The tall one saw the Catholic crumple down beside him and roll into the precipice; then the oldest of them fell with his head back and vanished, dragging his last cry down the walls of rock. Between the puffs of gunpowder he saw a peasant struggling with a blocked bolt, then he too fell into the darkness.

A cloud of pain in the back like a swarm of stinging bees prevented him losing consciousness at once; he had fallen through a briar-bush. Then tons of emptiness weighed down on his stomach, and he fainted.

Suddenly he seemed to be back on a height as if the earth had given a great heave; he had stopped. His fingers were wet and he smelled blood. He must be crushed to bits and about to die.

76

But he did not feel himself getting weaker and all the agonies of the fall were very lively and distinct in his mind. He tried to move a hand; the left one; it responded. He groped along the other arm, touched his pulse, his elbow; but the arm did not feel anything, it might have been dead, it only moved if raised by the other hand. He felt then that he was holding the wrist of his right arm in both hands; this was impossible. Then he realised that he was holding someone else's arm; he had fallen on the dead body of one of the other two. He prodded the fat flesh of the Catholic; that was the soft cushion which had broken his fall. That was why he was alive. That was why; and also, he remembered now, because he had not been hit but had flung himself down beforehand; he could not remember, though, if he had done it intentionally, but that was not important now. Then he discovered that he could see; some light was filtered down there in the depths and the tallest of the three naked men could make out his own hands and those sticking out of the heap of flesh beneath him. He turned and looked up; at the top was an aperture full of light; the opening of the Witch's Hole. First it hurt his eyes like a yellow flash; then they got used to it and he could see the blueness of the sky, far away from him, twice as far as the earth's crust.

The sight of the sky plunged him in despair; it would certainly be better to be dead. Now he was there with his two dead companions at the bottom of a very deep pit, from which he could never get out again. He shouted. The streak of sky above at the top became fringed with heads. " One of them's alive! " they said. They threw something down. The naked man watched it dropping like a stone, then hit against the wall, and heard an explosion. There was a niche in the rock behind him and the naked man squeezed into it; the well was full of dust and pieces of splintered rock. He pulled at the body of the Catholic and held it up in front of the niche; it only just kept together but was the only thing he could use to shelter himself. He was just in

77

time; another grenade came down and reached the bottom, raising a spray of blood and stones. The corpse broke up; now the naked man had no defence or hope. In the patch of sky appeared the white beard of the big old man. The others had drawn to one side.

"Hey!" called the big man with the beard.

"Hey!" replied the naked man, from the depths.

And the big man with the beard repeated: "Hey!"

There was nothing else to say between them.

Then the big man with the beard turned round. "Throw him a rope," he said.

The naked man did not understand. He saw some of the heads leaving and the ones remaining making signs at him, signs of agreement, not to worry. The naked man looked at them with his head stuck out of the niche, not daring to expose himself altogether, feeling the same disquiet as when he had been sitting on the stone during the trial. But the peasants were not throwing grenades any more, they were looking down and asking him questions, to which he replied with groans. The rope did not come, and one by one the peasants left the edge. The naked man then came out of his hiding-place and looked at the distance separating him from the top, the walls of sheer naked rock.

At that moment appeared the face of the haunted man. He was looking round and smiling. Then he moved back from the edge of the Witch's Hole; aimed his rifle into it and fired; the naked man heard the bullet whistle past his ear; the Witch's Hole was a narrow shaft and not quite vertical, so things thrown in rarely reached the bottom and bullets easily hit a layer of rock and stopped there. He squatted in his refuge, with foam on his lips, like a dog. Now up there all the peasants were back and one was unwinding a long rope down the shaft. The naked man watched the rope coming down but did not move.

"Hey!" the one with the black moustaches shouted down. "Catch hold of it and come up."

But the naked man was still in his niche.

"Come along; up with you, now," they shouted. "We won't do you any harm."

And they made the rope dance about in front of his eyes. The naked man was frightened.

"We won't do you any harm. We swear it," the men were saying, trying to sound sincere. And they were sincere; they wanted to save him at all costs so as to be able to shoot him all over again; but at that moment they just wanted to save him and their voices had a tone of affection, of human brotherhood.

The naked man sensed all this and anyway he had little choice; and he put a hand on the rope. But then among the men holding it he saw the head of the man with haunted eyes; and he dropped the rope and hid himself. They had to begin convincing him, begging him all over again; finally he decided and began going up. The rope was full of knots and it was easy to climb up it, and he could also catch hold of jutting bits of rock; so the naked man moved slowly up towards the light and saw the heads of the peasants at the top becoming clearer and bigger. Then the man with the haunted eyes reappeared all of a sudden and the others did not have time to hold him back; he was holding an automatic gun and began firing it at once. At the first burst the rope broke right above the naked man's hands. He crashed down, knocking against the sides, and fell back down on the remains of his companions. Up there, against the sky, he saw the big man with the beard moving his arms and shaking his head.

The others were trying to explain, by gestures and shouts, that it was not their fault, that they'd punish that madman, and that now they'd look for another rope and bring him up again. But the naked man had lost hope now; he would never be able to return to the earth's surface; he would never leave the bottom of this shaft, and would go mad there drinking blood and eating human flesh, without ever being able to die. Up there, against

79

the sky, there were good angels with ropes, and bad angels with grenades and rifles, and a big old man with a white beard who waved his arms but could not save him.

The armed men, seeing him unconvinced by their fair words, decided to finish him off with hand grenades, and began throwing them down. But the naked man had found another hiding-place, a narrow horizontal crack in the rock where he could slip in and be safe. At every grenade which fell he crawled deeper into this crack until he reached a point where he could not see any more light. He went on dragging himself along on his stomach like a snake, with darkness and the damp slimy rock all round him. From being damp the rock-surface beneath him was now getting wet, then covered with water; the naked man could feel the cold trickle running under his stomach. It was the way opened under the earth by the rains coming down from the Witch's Hole; a very long narrow cavern, a subterranean drain. Where would it end? Perhaps it would lose itself in blind caves in the belly of the mountain, perhaps it would funnel the water through narrow little channels which would issue into springs. And his body would rot away there in a drain and infect the waters of the springs, poisoning entire villages.

The air was almost unbreathable; the naked man felt the moment coming when his lungs could no longer resist. Instead of which the flow of water was increasing and getting deeper and quicker; the naked man was now slithering along with his whole body under water and could clean off the crust of mud and of his own and others' blood. He did not know if he had moved far or not; the complete darkness and that slithering movement had deprived him of all sense of distance. He was exhausted. In front of his eyes luminous shapeless forms were beginning to appear. The farther he advanced, the clearer these shapes became, took on definite, though continuously transforming edges. Supposing it was not just a dazzle inside the retina of his eyes, but a light, a real light, at the end of the cavern? He only had to close his eyes, or look in the opposite direction, to make certain. But anyone who gazes fixedly at a light has a dazzled feeling at the roots of his eyes even if he shuts his lids and turns his eyes round; so he could not distinguish between the light outside and the lights in his own eyes, and remained in doubt.

He noticed something else new, by touch; the stalactites. Slimy stalactites were hanging from the roof of the cave and stalagmites coming up from the ground on the verges of the water, where they were not eroded. The naked man began pulling himself along by these stalactites above his head. And as he moved he noticed that his arms from being folded to grasp the stalactites, were gradually straightening out, which meant that the cave was getting bigger. Soon the man could arch his back and walk on all fours; and the light was becoming less uncertain; he could tell now if his eyes were open or shut, he was beginning to make out the shapes of things, the arch of the roof, the droop of the stalactites, the black glitter of the current.

And finally he was walking upright, up the long cave towards the luminous opening, with the water to his waist, still hanging on to the stalactites, though, to keep himself straight. One stalactite seemed bigger than the others and when the man seized it he felt it opening in his hand and a cold soft wing beating on his face. A bat! It flew off, and the other bats hanging with their heads down woke up and flew away; soon the whole cave was full of silent flying bats, and the man felt the wind from their wings around him and their skin brushing against his forehead and mouth. He walked on in a cloud of bats until he reached the open air.

The cave came out into a torrent. Once again the naked man was on the crust of the earth, under the sky. Was he safe now? He must take care not to make any mistakes. The torrent was running silently over white and black stones. Around it was a wood full of twisted trees; all that grew in the undergrowth was thorns and brambles. He was naked in wild and deserted parts,

and the nearest human beings were enemies who would follow
him with pitchforks and guns as soon as they saw him.

The naked man climbed up a willow tree. The valley was all
woods and shrub-covered slopes, under a grey hump of mountain.
But at the end of it, where the torrent turned, there was a slate roof
with white smoke coming up. Life, thought the naked man, was
a hell, with rare moments recalling some ancient paradise.

Animal Wood

ON DAYS of Fascist round-ups the wood might have been a fairground. Off the paths among the bushes and trees there was a continuous passage of families urging along a cow or calf, and old women leading a goat on a rope, and girls with a goose under one arm. Some of them were even escaping with their rabbits.

Wherever one went, the thicker the chestnut woods, the more one ran into heavy-bellied bulls and tinkling cows, which were finding it difficult to move on those rocky slopes. Best off were the goats, but perhaps the happiest were the mules which just this once could move without a burden and go cropping leaves along the alleys. The pigs went rooting about in the ground, pricking their snouts all over with chestnut husks; the chickens roosted in the trees and frightened the squirrels; the rabbits, which after centuries of cages had forgotten how to dig themselves lairs, took refuge in hollow tree-trunks, where they were sometimes bitten by squirrels.

That morning a peasant called Giuà Dei Fichi was gathering fuel in a remote corner of the wood. He knew nothing about what was happening in the village, as he had left the evening before, intending to gather mushrooms in the morning, and had slept in the middle of the wood in a hut used, in autumn, for drying chestnuts.

So as he was chopping a dead tree-trunk with a hatchet he was surprised to hear a vague tinkling of bells far and near through the wood. He stopped chopping and heard voices getting closer. " Oo-u," he shouted.

Giuà Dei Fichi was a short tubby little man, with a face like a full moon, dark of skin and flushed with wine; he wore a green conical hat with a pheasant's feather stuck in it, a shirt with big yellow spots under a homespun jerkin, and a red scarf around his tubby stomach to hold up trousers covered with purple blotches.

" Coo-u! " came the reply, and between the green lichenous rocks appeared a close friend, a peasant with moustaches and a straw hat, dragging behind him a big goat with a white beard.

" What're you doing here, Giuà? " asked his friend. " The Germans've reached the village and are going round all the stalls! "

" Oh! " shouted Giuà Dei Fichi, " they'll find my cow Cochineal and take her off! "

" Hurry up and you may still be in time to hide her," advised his friend. " We saw the column as it was coming up through the valley and we made off at once. But they may not have reached your place yet."

Giuà left his hatchet and basket of mushrooms and rushed off. As he ran through the wood he met rows of ducks which scattered quacking between his feet, and flocks of sheep marching compactly side by side without moving to let him through, and children and old women who shouted: " They've reached the Madonnetta! They're searching the houses above the bridge! I've seen them turning the last corner before the village! " Giuà Dei Fichi quickened up his short legs, and went rolling down the slopes like a ball, and panting up the hills with his heart in his mouth.

On and on he ran till he reached a turn of a hill from which opened a view of the village. A great expanse of tender early morning air, a misty ring of hills, and in the middle the village, knobbly houses all stone and slate, heaped on top of each other. And through the thin air came the sounds of shouts in German and of fists banging against doors.

"Oh dear! The Germans are already in the houses!"

Giuà Dei Fichi was trembling all over his arms and legs; a bit of a tremor he already had from drinking and more now came over him at the thought of his cow Cochineal, the one possession he had in the world, about to be taken away from him.

Very quietly, cutting through fields, keeping under cover of vines, Giuà Dei Fichi drew near the village. His little house was one of the last, on the outskirts, in the middle of a green mass of pumpkins, where the village merged into vegetable patches; possibly the Germans might not have reached it yet.

Peeping round each corner, Giuà began slipping into the village. He saw an empty street with the usual smells of hay and stalls; those new noises were coming from the middle of the village—inhuman voices and stamping of iron-clad feet. There his house was—still shut up. The door of the stall on the ground floor was closed and so was that of the rooms at the top of the worn outside staircase, with its clumps of basil planted in cooking-pots filled with earth. A voice from the inside of the stall said: "Muuuuu" it was his cow Cochineal recognising the approach of her owner. Giuà blushed with pleasure.

But now from under an arcade resounded a tramp of feet; Giuà hid in a doorway, drawing in his round paunch. It was a German, with the look of a peasant, wrists and neck jutting out of his short tunic, and long, long legs and a big gun as long as himself. He had left the others to try and find something on his own; and also because the look and smells of the village reminded him of things and smells he knew well. So he was walking along sniffing the air and looking around with a yellow porkish face under the peak of his squashed cap. At that moment Cochineal lowed: "Muuu . . ." She could not understand why her master had not arrived yet. The German quivered in his shrunken clothes and at once made for the stall; Giuà Dei Fichi held his breath.

He saw the German beginning to kick violently at the door; he'd break it in soon, for sure. Then Giuà slipped round the corner behind the house, went to the haystack and began groping about under the hay. There he'd hidden his old double-barrelled shot-gun, with a full belt of cartridges. Giuà loaded the gun with a couple of shots, strapped the belt round his tummy, then very quietly, with the gun at the ready, went and hid behind the door of the stall.

The German was coming out pulling Cochineal along behind him on a rope. She was a fine red cow with black markings (that was why she was called Cochineal), a young, affectionate, punc-tilious cow; she did not want to be taken off by this man she did not know, and was hesitating; the German had to pull her along by the halter.

Giuà Dei Fichi looked on, hidden behind a wall. Now, it should be said that Giuà was the worst shot in the village. Never had he succeeded in hitting, even by mistake, I won't say a hare—but even a squirrel. When he shot at sitting thrushes, they didn't even bother to move from the branch. No one wanted to go shooting with him as he was apt to hit other men's behinds. He couldn't aim, as his hands always trembled.

He pointed the gun but his hands were trembling and the barrel of the shot-gun waved about in the air. He tried to aim at the German's heart, but what he saw through the sights was the cow's rump. "Oh dear!" thought Giuà, "suppose I fire at the German and kill Cochineal." So he didn't dare fire.

The German was moving along very slowly with this cow which could sense the nearness of her master and was refusing to be dragged. Suddenly he realised that his fellow-soldiers had already evacuated the village and were going away down the road. The German tried to catch them up, pulling that stubborn cow after him; and Giuà followed him at a distance, jumping behind bushes and walls and pointing his shot-gun every now and again. But he could not manage to keep the weapon steady, and the German and the cow were always too near each other for him to dare fire a shot. Must he let the German take her away?

To reach the column in the distance the German took a short cut through the woods. Now it was easier for Giuà to keep behind by hiding among the tree-trunks. And perhaps now the German would begin walking farther away from the cow so that it would be possible to shoot at him.

Once in the wood Cochineal seemed to lose her reluctance to move, and even, as the German was apt to get lost among the paths, which he could scarcely make out, began guiding him and deciding whenever two paths crossed. Before long the German realised he was not on the short cut to the main road but in the middle of a thick wood; both he and the cow were lost, in fact.

Giuà Dei Fichi, his nose scratched by branches, his feet soaked by rivulets he'd fallen into, was still following along behind, among flapping birds taking to flight and frogs croaking in the mud. It was even more difficult to aim among the trees, with all those obstacles around and that wine red and black rump which seemed always to be there under his eyes.

The German was already looking in alarm at the thickness of the wood and wondering how he could get out of it, when he heard a rustling in an arbutus bush and out came a fine red pig. At home he'd never seen pigs wandering about in the woods. He loosened the rope of the cow and began following the pig. As soon as Cochineal felt herself free she trotted off into the wood, which was, she sensed, full of friendly creatures.

Now was the moment for Giuà to shoot. The German was fussing round the pig, clutching it to keep it still, but it slipped away.

Giuà was just about to press the trigger, when nearby appeared two small children, a little boy and a little girl, wearing woollen caps with pom-poms and long stockings. Big tears were dropping from their eyes. " Aim carefully, Giuà, please," they said. " If you kill the pig we'll have nothing left! " Giuà Dei Fichi felt the gun dancing about in his hands again; he had such a tender heart and was too easily moved, not by having to kill that German but by having to risk the pig belonging to those two poor little children.

The German was swaying about among the rocks and bushes, gripping the pig, which was wriggling about and grunting: "Ghiii . . . ghiii . . . ghiii . . ." Suddenly the pig's grunts were answered by a "Beee . . ." and out from a cave trotted a little lamb. The German let the pig go and ran after the lamb. "What a strange wood," he thought, "with pigs in bushes and lambs in caves." And he caught the lamb, which was bleating at the top of its voice, by a leg, hitched it up on his shoulder like the Good Shepherd, and off he went. Very quietly Giuà Dei Fichi followed. "This time he won't escape. This time he's had it," he said to himself, and was just about to fire, when a hand raised the barrel of his gun. It was an old shepherd with a white beard, who was now holding out his joined hands towards him and saying: "Giuà, don't kill my little lamb, kill the German but don't kill my little lamb. Aim well, just this once, aim well!" But Giuà was completely confused by now, and couldn't even find the trigger.

The German on his way through the wood was making discoveries that left him open-mouthed: chickens perched on trees, guinea-pigs peering from hollow trunks. It was a complete Noah's Ark. Then he saw a turkey spreading its tail on the branch of a pine. At once he put up his hand to catch it, but the turkey gave a little skip and went and perched on a branch higher up, still spreading its tail. The German left the lamb and began climbing up the pine. But every layer of branches he reached, the turkey went up another layer, without looking in the least put out, still preening itself and with its hanging wattles aflame.

Giuà moved under the tree with a leafy branch on his head, two others on his shoulders and one tied to the barrel of his gun. But then a plump young woman with a red handkerchief tied round her head came up to him. "Giuà," she said, "listen to me. If you kill the German I'll marry you, if you kill the turkey I'll do you in." Giuà, who was still a bachelor though no longer young, and very modest, blushed scarlet and his gun began waving round like a turnspit.

The German was still climbing and had reached the smallest branches; then one of them broke under him and down he fell. He very nearly fell right on top of Giuà Dei Fichi, who did this time see straight and get away in time. But on the ground Giuà left all the branches that had been hiding him, so the German fell on them and did not hurt himself.

As he fell he saw a hare on the path. But no, it wasn't a hare; it was round and paunchy and did not run away when it heard a noise, but settled down on the ground. It was a rabbit; the German took it by the ears. He walked on with the rabbit wriggling and twisting about in all directions, so that in order not to let it escape he had to keep jumping about with his arm raised. The wood was full of lowing, bleating and screeching; at every step were new things to be seen: a parrot on a holly branch, three goldfish wriggling in a spring.

Giuà, from astride the high branch of an ancient oak, was following the German's dance with the rabbit. But it was difficult to aim at him because the rabbit was constantly changing position and getting in between. Giuà felt a pull at a corner of his jerkin; it was a little girl with plaits and a freckly face. "Don't kill the rabbit, Giuà, please; I don't mind about your shooting the German, though."

Meanwhile the German had reached a place which was covered with grey stones spotted with blue and green lichen. There were only a few bare pines growing there, and nearby opened a precipice. A hen was scratching about in the carpet of pine-needles covering the ground. The German began running after the hen and the rabbit escaped.

It was the thinnest, oldest and scraggiest hen he had ever seen. It belonged to Girumina, the poorest old woman in the village. Now the German had it in his hands.

Giuà was lying on top of the rocks and had constructed a pedestal of stones for his shot-gun. He had even put up a sort of little fortress, with only a narrow slit for the barrel. Now he could fire without having any scruples, as even if he killed that scraggy hen little harm was done.

But now old Girumina came up to him, wrapped in her ragged black shawls, and began saying persuasively: "Giuà, it's bad enough that a German should take away my hen, the last thing I possess in all the world. But it's much worse that you should be the one to kill it."

Giuà began trembling more than ever before because of the great responsibility weighing on him. But he pulled himself together and pressed the trigger.

The German heard the shot and saw the chicken wriggling in his hands lose its tail. Another shot, and the chicken lost a wing. Was it bewitched, this chicken, that it exploded every now and again and was falling to pieces in his hands? There was another explosion and the chicken was completely featherless, ready for roasting, and yet it still went on flapping its one wing. The German was beginning to be seized with terror and holding it away from him by the neck. Giuà's fourth cartridge cut the neck off right under his hand and left him holding the head, which was still moving. He flung it aside and ran away. But he could not find any more paths. Near him was that rocky precipice. The last tree before the precipice was a carob and on its branches the German saw a big cat crouching.

By now he was beyond feeling any surprise at seeing domestic animals scattered in the woods and he put out a hand to stroke the cat. Then he took it by the nape of the neck, hoping to please it and hear it purr.

For some time now that wood had been infested by a savage wild cat which killed birds and sometimes even got into the hen-coops in the village. So the German, who was expecting to hear it purr, suddenly saw the cat fling itself at him with its fur on end, and felt its nails slashing into him. In the struggle which followed both man and beast rolled over the edge of the precipice.

So it was that Giuà, a hopeless shot, was fêted as the greatest partisan and huntsman in the village. And poor Girumina was bought a brood of newly-hatched chicks at the expense of the community.

Seen in the Canteen

I KNEW at once that something would happen. The two were looking at each other across the table with expressionless eyes, like fish in an aquarium. But one could see that they were strangers and quite incomprehensible to each other, two unknown animals, each watching and distrusting the other.

She had arrived first; a huge woman in black, obviously a widow —a widow from the country up in town on business was how I placed her as soon as I saw her. Her kind of people also came to the popular 60-*lire* canteen where I ate: black marketeers, big and small operators alike, with a taste for economy remaining with them from their days of poverty, but with sporadic outbursts of extravagance every now and again when they remembered that their pockets were full of 1,000-*lire* notes—outbursts that made them order spaghetti and beefsteak, while we others, thin bachelors eating on meal tickets, eyed them enviously and gulped down spoonfuls of vegetable soup. The woman must have been quite a rich marketeer; she sat down, occupying a whole side of the table, and began pulling out of her bag pieces of white bread, fruit, carelessly wrapped cheese, and spreading them all over the cloth. Then, with her black-rimmed fingers, she began mechanically picking at grapes and bits of bread, and shovelling them into her mouth, where they vanished in a slow chewing motion.

It was at this moment that he approached and saw the empty

chair at a still uncluttered corner of the table. He bowed. "May I?" The woman glanced up and went on chewing. He tried again. "Excuse me—may I?" The woman shrugged her shoulders and let out a grunt from a mouth full of chewed bread. The man raised his hat slightly and sat down. He was an old man, neat but rather shabby, with a starched collar, wearing an overcoat although it was not winter; a flex from a deaf-aid instrument hung from his ear. I felt sorry for him at once, sorry for the air of good breeding emanating from his every gesture. He was obviously a gentleman who had come down in the world, fallen suddenly from a world of compliments and bows to one of shoves and digs in the ribs, without ever understanding how it had all happened but continuing to bow among the crowd in the canteen as if he were at a court reception.

Now they were face to face, the newly-rich woman and the ex-rich man, animals unknown one to the other; the woman broad and short with her large hands resting on the table like the claws of a crab, and breathing as if she had a crab in her throat too; the old man sitting on the edge of his chair with his arms pressed against his sides, his gloved hands paralysed with arthritis, and little blue veins protruding from his face, like lichen on a red stone.

"Excuse my hat," he said. The woman looked at him out of the yellows of her eyes. She understood nothing about him at all.

"Excuse me," repeated the man, "for keeping my hat on. There's rather a draught."

The large widow smiled then, at the corners of her mouth, covered with soft down like an insect's; a stiffened smile, almost without moving a muscle of her face, like a ventriloquist's.

"Wine," she said to a passing waitress.

At that word the eyes of the old man with the gloves flickered; he obviously liked his wine, the veins at the top of his nose bore witness to the long careful drinking of a gourmet. But he must have given up drinking for some time. The widow was now

93

dropping pieces of white bread into her glass of wine and still chewing steadily.

Perhaps the old man with the gloves suddenly felt a pang of shame, as if he were courting a woman and was afraid of appearing mean. "Wine for me too!" he called.

Then at once he seemed to have repented of saying this; perhaps he thought that if he finished his pension before the end of the month he would have to starve for days, muffled in his overcoat in his cold attic. He did not pour the wine into his glass. "Perhaps," he thought, "if I don't touch it I can give it back, say I no longer want it, then I won't have to pay for it."

And, indeed, the desire for wine had already passed, as had also the desire to eat; he rattled his spoon in the tasteless soup, chewing with his few remaining teeth, while the large widow swallowed forkfuls of macaroni dripping in butter.

"Let's hope they'll be quiet now," I thought. "That one or the other will finish soon and go." I don't know what I was afraid of. Each of them were monstrous beings in their way, and under their slow crustacean-like appearances both were charged with a reciprocal terrible hatred. I imagined a battle between them like a slow tearing to pieces of monsters at the bottom of the sea.

The old man was already surrounded, almost besieged, by the wrappings from the widow's food scattered over the table; confined to a corner with his tasteless soup and his two poor coupon rolls, he tried to pull them nearer as if afraid they would get lost in the enemy camp, but with an involuntary move of his gloved and paralysed hand he pushed a piece of cheese off the table, and it fell to the ground.

The widow seemed to loom up in front of him more enormous than ever; she was grinning. "Excuse me . . . excuse me," said the old man with the gloves. She looked at him as one looks at a new kind of animal, but did not reply.

"Now," I thought. "Now he'll shout out 'Enough of this'—and tear off the tablecloth!"

Instead he bent down, and with clumsy movements searched for the cheese under the table. The big widow stopped, looked at him for a moment, then almost without moving dropped one of her enormous paws to the floor, picked up the piece of cheese, brushed it, popped it into her insect's mouth, and had swallowed it before the old man with the gloves re-emerged.

Finally he straightened up, aching with the effort, red with confusion, his hat crooked and the flex of his hearing aid awry.

"Now," I thought. "Now he'll take up a knife and kill her!"

Instead, however, he seemed unable to console himself for the unfavourable impression he felt he had created. Obviously he longed to talk, to say anything at all to dispel the uncomfortable atmosphere. But he could not think of a single phrase that did not refer to the incident, did not sound like an excuse.

"That cheese," he said. "Such a pity, really—I'm so sorry . . ."

The large widow did not just want to humiliate him by her silence, she wanted to squash him completely.

"Oh, it doesn't matter at all," she said. "At Castel Brandone I've got cheeses this size," and she moved her hands apart. But it was not the space between her hands that impressed the old man.

"Castel Brandone?" he said, and his eyes lit up. "I was at Castel Brandone as a second lieutenant! In '95; for the shooting. If you come from there, you must know the Counts of Brandone d'Asprez!"

The widow was not just grinning now, she was laughing. Laughing and turning round to see if any others had noticed this ridiculous old man.

"You wouldn't remember," went on the old man. "You certainly wouldn't remember—but that year at Castel Brandone, for the shooting, the King came! There was a reception at the

95

d'Asprez' castle. And it was there that what I am about to tell
you happened."

The large widow looked at her watch, ordered a plate of liver
and began hurriedly eating, without listening to him. The old
man with the gloves knew that he was talking to himself, but he
did not stop; it would have made a bad impression to stop, he
must finish the story he had begun.

" His Majesty entered the brilliantly lit drawing-room," he continued with tears in his eyes, " and on one side were the ladies in
evening dress curtseying, and on the other us officers standing at
attention. And the King kissed the countess's hand and greeted
first one and then another. Then he came up to me . . ."

The two quarter-litre bottles of wine were side by side on the
table; that of the widow almost finished, that of the old man
still full. Without thinking the widow poured some wine out of
the full bottle and drank it. The old man noticed this, even in the
heat of his story-telling; now there was no more hope, he would
have to pay for it. And perhaps the widow would drink it all.
But it would be impolite to point out her mistake, and besides it
might hurt her feelings. No, it would be too indelicate.

" And His Majesty asked me: ' And you, Lieutenant?' Just
like that he asked. And I, standing at attention: ' Second
Lieutenant Clermont de Fronges, Your Majesty.' And the King
said: ' Clermont! I knew your father; a fine soldier!' And he
shook my hand . . . Just like that he said it: ' A fine soldier!'"

The large widow had finished eating and got up. Now she
was rummaging in her bag which was propped on the other chair.
She bent over the chair and all that could be seen above the table
was her behind, an enormous fat woman's behind, covered in
black. Old Clermont de Fronges was facing this big waggling
behind. He went on telling his story, his face transfigured: " The
whole room brilliant with chandeliers and mirrors. And the King
shaking me by the hand. ' Bravo, Clermont de Fronges,' he said
to me . . . and the ladies all standing round in evening dress . . ."

Theft in a Cake Shop

WHEN DRITTO got to the place they were to meet, the others had already been waiting some time. There were two of them, Baby and Uora-Uora. The street was so silent that the ticking of the clocks could be heard in the houses. With two jobs to do, they'd have to hurry if they were to get through them by dawn.

" Come on," said Dritto.

" Where to? " they asked.

But Dritto was never one to explain about any job he was going to do.

" Come on now," he replied.

And he walked along in silence, through streets empty as dry rivers, with the moon following them along the tram-lines, Dritto ahead, gazing round with those yellow restless eyes of his and moving his nostrils as if they were smelling something peculiar.

Baby was called that because he had a big head like a new-born baby and a stumpy body; also perhaps because of his short hair and pretty little face with small black moustaches. He was all muscle and moved so softly he might have been a cat; there was no one like him at climbing up walls and squeezing through openings, and Dritto always had good reason to take him along.

" Will it be a good job, Dritto? " asked Baby.

" If we bring it off," answered Dritto, a reply which didn't mean much.

Meanwhile, by a devious route which only he knew, he had led them round a corner into a yard. The other two soon realised that they were going to work on the back of a shop, and Uora-Uora pushed ahead in case he was left as look-out. It always fell to Uora-Uora to be look-out man; he longed to break into houses, search around and fill his pockets like the others, but he always found himself standing guard on cold streets, in danger from police patrols, his teeth chattering in the cold, and chain-smoking to calm his nerves. He was an emaciated Sicilian, Uora-Uora, with a sad mulatto face and wrists jutting out of his sleeves. When on a job he always dressed up in his best, God knows why, complete with hat, tie and raincoat, and if forced to run for it, he'd snatch up the ends of his raincoat as if spreading wings.

"You're look-out, Uora-Uora," said Dritto, dilating his nostrils. Uora-Uora went off quietly; he knew Dritto and the danger signal of those dilating nostrils, which would move quicker and quicker until they suddenly stopped and he whipped out a revolver.

"There," Dritto said to Baby. He pointed to a little window high off the ground, covered with a piece of cardboard in place of a broken pane.

"You climb up, get in and open for me," he said. "Take care not to put on the lights as they'll be seen from outside."

Baby pulled himself up on the smooth wall like a monkey, pushed in the cardboard without a sound, and stuck his head through. It was then that he became aware of the smell; he took a deep breath and up through his nostrils wafted an aroma of freshly baked cakes. It gave him a feeling of shy excitement, of remote tenderness, rather than of actual greed.

"Oh, what a lot of cakes there must be in here," he thought. It was years since he had eaten a proper bit of cake, not since before the war perhaps. He decided to search around till he found them. He jumped down into the darkness, kicked against a telephone, got a broomstick up his trouser-leg, and then hit the ground. The smell of cakes was stronger than ever, but he couldn't tell where it was coming from.

" Yes, there must be a lot of cakes in here," thought Baby.

He reached out a hand, trying to feel his way in the dark, so as to reach the door and open it for Dritto. Quickly he recoiled in horror; he must be face to face with some animal, some soft, slimy sea-thing, perhaps. He stood there with his hand in the air, a hand that had suddenly become damp and sticky, as if covered with leprosy. Between the fingers had sprouted something round and soft, an excrescence, a tumour perhaps. He strained his eyes in the dark but could see nothing, not even when he put his hand under his nose. But he could smell, even though he could not see; and he burst out laughing. He realised he had touched a tart and was holding a blob of cream and a crystallised cherry.

At once he began licking the hand, and groping around with the other at the same time. It touched something solid but soft, with a thin covering of fine sugar; a doughnut! Still groping, he popped the whole of it into his mouth and gave a little cry of pleasure on discovering it had jam inside. It really was the most wonderful place; whatever way he stretched his hand out in the darkness, it found new kinds of cakes.

He was suddenly aware of an impatient knocking on a door nearby; it was Dritto waiting to be let in. Baby moved towards the sound and his hands bumped first into a meringue and then into an almond cake. He opened the door and Dritto's torch lit up his little face with its moustaches already white with cream.

" It's full of cakes, here!" exclaimed Baby, as if the other did not know.

" This isn't a time for cakes," said Dritto, pushing him aside. " We've got to hurry." And he went ahead twisting the beam of his torch round in the dark. Everywhere it touched it lit up rows of shelves, and on the shelves rows of trays, and on the trays rows of cakes of every conceivable shape and colour, tarts filled with cream glittering like candle wax, and piles of sugar-coated buns and castles of almond cakes.

It was then that a terrible worry came over Baby; the worry of not having time to eat all he wanted, of being forced to make his escape before he had sampled all the different kinds of cakes, of having all this land of milk and honey at his disposal only for a few minutes in his whole life. And the more cakes he discovered, the more his anxiety increased, and every new corner and every fresh view of the shop that was lit up by Dritto's torch seemed to be about to shut him off.

He flung himself on the shelves, choking himself with cakes, cramming two or three inside his mouth at a time, without even tasting them; he seemed to be battling with the cakes, as if they were threatening enemies, strange monsters besieging him, a crisp and sticky siege which he must break through by the force of his jaw. The slit halves of the big sugared buns seemed to be opening yellow throats and eyes at him, the cream-horns to be blossoming like flowers of carnivorous plants; for a horrible moment Baby had the feeling that it was he who was being devoured by the cakes.

Dritto pulled him by the arm. " The till," he said. "We've got to open the till."

At the same time, as he passed, he stuffed a piece of multi-coloured sponge into his mouth, a cherry off a tart and then a brioche, hurriedly as if anxious not to be distracted from the job on hand. He had switched off his torch.

" From outside they could see us quite clearly," he said.

They had now reached the front of the cakeshop with its show-cases and marbled top counters. Through the grilled shutters the lights from the street came in streaks, and could be seen outside casting strange shadows on the trees and houses.

Now the moment had come to force the till.

" Hold this," said Dritto, handing the torch to Baby with the beam pointing downwards so that it could not be seen from outside.

But Baby was holding the torch with one hand and groping around with the other. He seized an entire plum cake, and while Dritto was busy at the lock with his tools, began chewing it as if it were a loaf of bread. But he soon tired of it and left it half eaten on the marble slab.

" Get away from there! Look what a filthy mess you're making," hissed Dritto through clenched teeth; in spite of his trade he had a strange respect for tidy work. Then he, too, couldn't resist the temptation and stuffed two biscuits, the kind that were half sponge and half chocolate, into his mouth, without interrupting his work though.

Now Baby, in order to have both hands free, had constructed a kind of lampshade from tray cloths and pieces of nougat. He then espied some large cakes with " Happy Birthday " written on them. He moved round them, studying the plan of attack; first he reviewed them with a finger and licked off a bit of chocolate cream, then he buried his face inside and began biting them from the middle one by one.

But he still felt a kind of frenzy which he did not know how to satisfy; he could not discover any way of enjoying everything completely. Now he was crouching on all fours over a table laden with tarts; he would have liked to lie down in those tarts, cover himself with them and never have to leave them. But five or ten minutes from now it would be all over; for the rest of his life cakeshops would be out of bounds to him again, for ever, like when he was a child squashing his nose against the window-pane. If only, at least, he could stay there three or four hours. . . .

" Dritto," he exclaimed. " Suppose we hide here till dawn, who'll see us? "

" Don't be a fool," said Dritto, who had now succeeded in forcing the till and was searching round among the notes. " We've got to get out of here before the cops arrive."

Just at that moment they heard a knock on the window. In the dim moonlight Uora-Uora could be seen knocking on the blind and making signs to them. The two in the shop gave a jump, but Uora-Uora motioned for them to keep calm and for Baby to come out and take his place, so that he could come in. The other two shook their fists and showed their teeth at him and made signs for him to get away from the front of the shop, if he didn't want his brains blown out.

Dritto, however, had found only a few thousand *lire* in the till, and was cursing and blaming Baby for not trying to help him. But Baby seemed beside himself; he was biting into doughnuts, picking at raisins, licking syrups, plastering himself all over and leaving sticky marks on the showcases and counters. He found that he no longer had any desire for cakes, in fact a feeling of nausea was beginning to creep up from the pit of his stomach, but he refused to believe it, he simply could not give up yet. And the doughnuts began to turn into soggy pieces of sponge, the tarts to flypaper and the cakes to asphalt. Now he saw only the corpses of cakes lying putrifying on their marble slabs, or felt them disintegrating like turgid glue inside his stomach.

Dritto was now cursing and swearing at the lock on another till, forgetful of cakes and hunger. Suddenly from the back of the shop appeared Uora-Uora swearing in his Sicilian dialect, which was quite unintelligible to either of them.

" The cops? " they asked, already pale.

" Change of guard! Change of guard! " Uora-Uora was croaking in his dialect, trying hard to explain how unjust it was to leave him starving out in the cold while they guzzled cakes inside.

" Go back and keep guard, go and keep guard! " shouted Baby angrily, the nausea from having eaten too much making him feel savage and selfish.

Dritto knew that it was only fair to Uora-Uora to make the change, but he also knew that Baby would not be convinced so easily, and without someone on guard they couldn't stay. So he pulled out his revolver and pointed it at Uora-Uora.

"Back to your post at once, Uora-Uora," he said.

Desperately, Uora-Uora thought of getting some supplies before leaving, and gathered a small pile of little almond cakes with nuts on them in his big hands.

"And suppose they catch you with your hands full of cakes, you fool, what'll you tell them?" Dritto swore at him. "Leave them all there and get out."

Uora-Uora burst into tears. Baby felt he hated him. He picked up a cake with "Happy Birthday" written on it and flung it in his face. Uora-Uora could easily have avoided it, instead of which he stuck his face out to get the full force, then burst out laughing, as his face, hat and tie were all covered in cream cake. Off he went, licking himself right up to his nose and cheeks.

At last Dritto succeeded in forcing the till and was stuffing all the notes he could find into his pocket, cursing because they stuck to his jammy fingers.

"Come on, Baby, time to go," he said.

But Baby could not leave just like that; this was a feast to be talked over for years to come with his cronies and with Tuscan Mary. Tuscan Mary was Baby's girl-friend; she had long smooth legs and a face and body that were almost horse-like. Baby liked her because he could curl himself up and wind round her like a cat.

Uora-Uora's second entry interrupted the course of these thoughts. Dritto quickly pulled out his revolver, but Uora-Uora shouted "The cops!" and rushed off, flapping the ends of his raincoat. Dritto gathered up the last few notes and was at the door in a couple of leaps; and Baby behind.

Baby was still thinking of Tuscan Mary and it was then that he remembered he might have taken her some cakes; he never gave her a present and she might make a scene about it. He went back, snatched up some cream-rolls, thrust them under his shirt, then quickly thinking that he had chosen the most fragile ones, looked around for something more solid and stuffed those into his bosom too. At that moment he saw the shadows of policemen moving on the window, waving their arms and pointing at something at the end of the street; and one of them aimed a revolver in that direction and fired.

Baby squatted down behind a counter. The shot did not seem to have hit its target; now they were making angry gestures and peering inside the shop. Shortly after he heard them finding the little door open, and then coming in. Now the shop was teeming with armed policemen. Baby remained crouched there, but meanwhile he found some candied fruit within arm's reach and chewed at slivers of citron and bergamot to calm his nerves.

The police had now discovered the theft and also found the remains of half-eaten cakes on the shelves. And so, distractedly, they, too, began to nibble little cakes that were lying about, taking care, though, to leave the traces of the thieves. After a few moments, becoming more enthusiastic in their search for evidence, they were all eating away heartily.

Baby was chewing, but the others were chewing even more loudly and drowned the sound. All of a sudden he felt a thick liquid oozing up from between his skin and his shirt, and a mounting nausea from his stomach. He was so dizzy with candied fruit that it was some time before he realised that the way to the door was free. The police described later how they had seen a monkey with its nose plastered with cream swing across the shop, overturning trays and tarts; and how by the time that they had recovered from their amazement and cleared the tarts from under their feet, he had escaped.

When Baby got to Tuscan Mary's and opened his shirt, he found his whole chest covered with a strange sticky paste. And they stayed till morning, he and she, lying on the bed licking and picking at each other till they had finished the last crumb of cake and blob of cream.

Dollars and the Demi-Mondaine

IT WAS after supper and Emanuele was flicking a flyswatter against the window-pane. He was thirty-two years old and plump. His wife, Jolanda, was changing her stockings to go out.

Through the window could be seen the rubble patch where the old warehouse used to be; across it opened a view of the sea, between houses sloping downhill; the sea was darkening, and a slow wind was surging up through the streets. Six sailors from the *Shenandoah*, an American torpedo-boat anchored outside the port, entered a tavern called The Tub of Diogenes.

" There are six Americans at Felice's," said Emanuele.

" Officers? " asked Jolanda.

" Sailors. Better. Hurry up." He pushed back his hat, and twisted round, groping for the sleeve of his jacket.

Jolanda had fastened her garter and was now tucking in the ribbons of her brassière which were sticking out in front.

" Ready? Let's go."

They trafficked in dollars, and so wanted to ask the sailors if they had any to sell; they were a respectable pair, though, for all their trafficking.

On the deserted rubble patch an odd palm-tree or two planted there to improve the area was rustling in the wind, as if desolate and disconsolate. And in the middle of the patch stood the brightly-lit construction called The Tub of Diogenes, put up by an ex-Serviceman called Felice, with the Town Council's permission and in spite of protests that it spoilt the neighbourhood. It was shaped like a barrel; inside was a bar and tables.

Emanuele turned to Jolanda. "Now, you go in first and start talking to them, and ask them if they'd like to change any dollars. They're more likely to say 'Yes' to you at once. Then I'll come in and clinch the deal."

A strategist, Emanuele. Off Jolanda went.

At Felice's the six sailors were lined along the bar from end to end, and all those white trousers and elbows leaning on the marble made it seem as if there were twelve of them. Jolanda approached and saw twelve eyes fixed on her, rotating in time with closed, chewing, grunting mouths. Most of them, in loose white tunics and with those caps perched on their heads, looked overgrown yet badly developed; but there was one near her, over six feet tall, with apple cheeks and a neck like a pyramid, whose uniform moulded him as if he were naked; he had a pair of round eyes with pupils that revolved to and fro without ever touching the lids. Jolanda hid a ribbon on her brassière which kept popping out.

From behind the bar, Felice, a chef's hat perched above swollen, sleepy eyes, was busy refilling glasses and seeing that all went well. From his cobbler's face, its chin perpetually dark in spite of shaving, came a grin of greeting. He spoke English, Felice did, and Jolanda whispered: "Felice, just ask them, will you, if they want to change any dollars?"

Felice, for ever grinning and evasive, replied: "Ask 'em yourself," and he told a young waiter with tar-black hair and an onion-coloured face to bring out more trays of *pizza* and chips.

Jolanda was now surrounded by those long, white chewing figures, exchanging inhuman grunts as they watched her.

"Please," she said in English, gesticulating. "Me to you *lire*, you to me dollars?"

They went on chewing. The big one with the bull neck smiled; he had the whitest teeth, so white that no gaps showed between.

A broad, short sailor, with a face as dark as a Spaniard's, now came towards her.

" Me to you dollars," he said in Italian, also gesticulating. " You to me bed."

Then he repeated it all in English, and the others gave long muffled laughs, still chewing and keeping their eyes fixed upon her.

Jolanda turned towards Felice. " Felice," she said, " explain to them."

" Whisky and soda," said Felice in his peculiar English, rolling some glasses on the marble top of the bar. His grin would have been nasty if he had not sounded so sleepy.

Then the giant sailor spoke; his voice rang out like an iron ring on a buoy buffeted by waves. He ordered Jolanda a drink, then took the glass from Felice's hand and held it out to her; it seemed incredible that the fragile stem of the glass didn't break in those huge fingers.

Jolanda did not know what to do. " Me *lire*, you dollars," she repeated.

But the others had already learnt Italian. " You bed," they cried. " Bed, dollars."

At this moment in came the husband, saw the circle of restless backs, and heard his wife's voice coming from somewhere in the middle of them. He went up to the bar. " Hey, Felice, tell me, will you . . ." he began.

" What can I get you ? " asked Felice with his tired grin. His chin, shaved only two hours ago, was already getting stubbly.

Emanuele tipped his hat back from his sweating forehead and began making little jumps to try and see over the wall of backs.

" My wife—what's she doing ? "

Felice climbed on a bench, stuck out his chin, then jumped down. " She's still in there," he replied.

Emanuele loosened the knot of his tie a little to breathe more freely.

" Tell her to come out," he said.

But Felice was busy scolding the onion-faced boy for leaving dishes without chips on them.

"Jolanda?" called her husband, and tried to push in between two Americans; he got a dig on the chin and another in the stomach, and was soon out, jumping up and down round the group again. From the thick of it all a rather tremulous little voice replied: "Emanuele?"

He shouted back: "How's it going . . ."

"It looks," said her voice, as if she were talking on the telephone, "It looks as if they don't want *lire* . . ."

He kept his calm, but was drumming on the counter. "They don't?" he cried. "Then come on out."

"Coming," she replied, and tried to make a little dive through that hedge of men. But there was something holding her back; she glanced down and saw a big hand placed against her, a big strong, gentle hand. In front of her was standing the giant with the apple cheeks, his teeth gleaming like the whites of his eyes.

"Please . . ." she begged softly, trying to loosen his hand, and calling out to Emanuele. "Just coming . . ." Instead she stayed there in the middle of them.

"Please," she kept on repeating. "Please."

Felice put a glass under Emanuele's nose.

"What can I get you?" he asked, lowering his head in its chef's hat, and leaning on the bar with his ten fingers splayed out.

Emanuele was staring into space. "Wait . . . I've an idea . . . Wait," he said and left.

Outside the street lamps were already lit. Emanuele ran across the street, went into the Café Lamarmora and looked all round. But there were just the regulars playing cards. "Come and join us, Manuele," they called out. "What's up, Manuele?" But he had already hurried out; on he ran without stopping till he reached the Paris Bar. He made a round of the tables, beating a fist against the palm of his hand. Finally he whispered in the barman's ear. The man said: "Not here yet—later to-night, maybe."

Emanuele hurried out. The barman burst out laughing and went over to tell the cashier.

At Giglio's La Bolognese, the old tart from Bologna, had hardly stretched out her legs under the table—her varicose veins were beginning to hurt—when Emanuele arrived with his cap on the back of his head, panting so hard she could not understand what he wanted.

" Come along," he cried, pulling her by the hand. " Come along, quick, it's urgent."

" Manuelino, boy, what's up with you? " asked La Bolognese, opening wide eyes surrounded by latticed wrinkles under a black fringe. " After all these years. . . . What *is* up with you, dearie? "

But he was already pulling her along by the hand, and she was hobbling behind, her swollen legs hampered by the tight petticoat half-way up her thighs.

In front of the cinema they ran into Mad Maria accosting a corporal.

" Hey, you, come along too. I'll take you to some Americans."

Mad Maria did not need telling twice; she left the corporal with a flick of a finger and started running along beside Emanuele, her red hair flying in the wind and her eyes piercing the darkness with anticipation.

The situation had not changed much in The Tub of Diogenes. There were several empty bottles on Felice's shelf, the gin had all gone, and the *pizze* just finishing. The two women bustled in with Emanuele urging them along from behind; the sailors found them suddenly pushed into their midst, and shouted cries of greeting. Exhausted, Emanuele slumped on to a stool. Felice poured him out a stiff drink. One of the sailors broke away from the group and came and slapped Emanuele on the back, while the others were giving friendly glances in his direction. Felice began telling them something about Emanuele.

" Well," asked Emanuele. " How d'you think it's going? "

Felice gave his eternal sleepy grin.

" Oh, you'll need at least six . . ."

Things were not improving, in fact; Mad Maria was hanging round the neck of a lanky sailor with a face like a fœtus, and squirming round in her green dress like a snake trying to change its skin; La Bolognese had the short Spaniard buried in her bosom and was cosetting him in a motherly way.

But Jolanda did not appear. That enormous back, always in front, prevented anyone seeing her. Emanuele made nervous signs to Mad Maria and La Bolognese to keep moving around, but they seemed oblivious to everything.

" Oooh . . ." said Felice, glancing over Emanuele's shoulders.

" What's that ? " he asked, but the barman was busy scolding the boy for not drying the glasses quickly enough. Emanuele turned round and saw more sailors arriving. There must have been fifteen of them. The Tub of Diogenes was soon full of drunken sailors. Mad Maria and La Bolognese flung themselves into the middle of the mêlée; Maria was jumping from one sailor's neck to the other, swirling her monkey legs in the air, and the other, with a constant false smile painted in lipstick, was gathering the lost ones to her breast like a broody hen.

Once Emanuele caught a sudden glimpse of Jolanda milling about in the midst of it all, then she vanished again. Every now and then Jolanda felt she was going to be trampled underfoot by the crowd round her, but each time she found beside her the giant sailor with the flashing white teeth and eyes, and each time she felt safe without knowing why. Moving softly, the man always kept beside her; his big body in its tight white uniform must have had muscles as smooth as a cat's; his chest rose and fell slowly, as if full of the great air of the sea. Suddenly that voice of his which boomed like a buoy began producing words one by one in a peculiar rhythm; he burst out into song, and they all began swaying and turning as if to a dance band.

Meanwhile, Mad Maria, who knew every corner of the place, was pushing and kicking her way towards a small door at the back of the bar, arm-in-arm with a sailor with a moustache. At first Felice did not want this door to be opened, but the whole mass of them were pushing behind and finally burst it in.

Emanuele, crouching on top of his stool, was following the scene with misty eyes.

" What's in there, Felice? What's in there?" But Felice did not reply, as he was worrying because there was nothing more to eat or drink.

" Go to Valkyria's and ask 'em to lend us something to drink," he said to the onion-faced lad. " Anything, even beer. And cakes. Hurry now."

During this time, Jolanda had been pushed through the little door. Inside was a small room, curtained and clean, with a bed in it, all made-up, with blue coverlet, wash-basin and everything èlse. Then the giant began to turn the others out of the room, calmly and firmly, pushing at them with his big hands, and keeping Jolanda behind his shoulders. But for some reason or other all the sailors wanted to stay in the little room, and at each wave that the giant sailor repulsed another wave returned—lessening each time, though, as some tired and stayed outside. Jolanda was pleased that the giant was doing this, as she was able to breathe more freely and also hide the ribbons which kept popping out of her brassière.

Emanuele was watching it all; he saw the giant's hands pushing the others out of the door, and his wife vanish so that she must certainly be inside, and the other sailors returning again and again in waves with one or two less in each wave; first ten, then nine, then seven. How many minutes would it take for the giant to succeed in shutting the door?

Then Emanuele hurried outside again. He crossed the square in hops, as if in a sack race. There was a line of taxis in the rank with all the drivers asleep. He went from one to another, waking them and explaining what he wanted them to do, furious if they didn't understand. One by one the taxis drove off in different directions. Emanuele went off in a taxi too, standing on the running-board.

The noise woke Baci, the old cabman on top of his box, and he hurried down to see if there was any fare to take. He quickly grasped the situation, like the old hand at the job he was, clambered back on his box and woke up his old horse. When Baci's cab had gone creaking off, the square was left deserted and silent, save for the noise coming from The Tub of Diogenes in the middle of the rubble patch.

At Iris's the girls were all dancing; they were very young, with bud-like mouths and tight jerseys moulding their jutting breasts. Emanuele was in too much of a hurry to wait till the dance ended. "Hey, you," he called to a girl dancing with her back pressed against a man whose hands were around her. The man turned towards Emanuele; he was a porter with hair low on his forehead and an open shirt. "What d'you want?" he exclaimed. Another three or four stopped around him: boxer's faces, breathing hard through their noses. "Let's get out," muttered Emanuele's driver, "or there'll be another row here too."

They went off to the Panther's place: but she didn't want to open up as she already had a client. "Dollars," shouted Emanuele, "dollars." She opened then, wrapped in a dressing-gown, looking like an allegorical statue. They dragged her down the stairs and pushed her into the taxi. Then they picked up Babilla walking along the sea front with her dog on a lead, Belbambin at the Traveller's Café with her fox fur round her neck, and Bekuana at the Hotel Pace with her ivory cigarette holder. At the Ninfea they found the proprietress had three new girls, who were giggling away and thought they were being taken for a ride in the country. They were all loaded in. Emanuele was sitting in front, rather overcome by the uproar made by all those women crushed in at the back; the taxi-driver was only worrying if the springs would hold.

Suddenly a figure ran into the middle of the road as if wanting to be run over. He made signs for them to stop; it was the onion-faced boy, loaded with a crate of beer and a tray of cakes, wanting a lift. The door flew open and with a gasp the boy vanished inside, beer, cakes and all. Off the taxi started again. Passers-by stopped and stared after this taxi racing along as if it were going to a casualty station, with those screams and high voices coming from inside. Every now and again Emanuele heard a long squeak and said to the driver: " Something's broken—can't you hear that noise ? "

The driver shook his head. " It's the boy," he said. Emanuele wiped the sweat from his brow.

When the taxi pulled up in front of the Tub, the boy jumped out first with the tray above his head and the crate under his other arm. His hair was standing on end, his eyes were open so wide they took up half his face, and he hopped away like a monkey.

" Felice," he cried. " Everything's safe! I didn't let them take a thing! But oh, if you knew what they did to me, Felice! "

Jolanda was still inside the little room, and the giant was still busy pushing sailors away from the door. But by now there was only one left who insisted on trying to get in; he was completely drunk and bounced back every time on the giant's hands. At this moment the new arrivals made their entry; Felice, wearily sur-veying the scene from the top of a stool, saw the sea of white caps part and a plumed hat, a shoulder covered in black silk, a fat haunch like a pig's, a breast draped with artificial flowers, swirling up to the surface and vanishing again like bubbles of air.

There was a sound of brakes outside, and four, five, six—an entire line of taxis arrived; and from every taxi emerged women. There was the Wriggler with her ladylike hair style, advancing majestically, screwing up her short-sighted eyes; there was Spanish Carmen swathed in veils, her face hollow as a skull, twisting her bony hips like a cat; there was old Lame Joan, hobbling on her little Chinese umbrella; there was the Black Girl of Long Alley with her negress' hair and furry legs; there was the Mouse in a dress covered with designs of cigarette brands; there was Milena the drug addict, in a dress patterned with playing cards; there was Lollypop with her face full of spots; and Ines the Femme Fatale in an all-lace gown.

Wheels could be heard crunching along the gravel: it was Baci's old cab with the horse half dead; he stopped and a woman jumped out from that too. She had a full velvet skirt trimmed with bows and lace, a bosom roped in necklaces, a black band round her throat, dangling ear-rings, a lorgnette, and a blonde wig topped by a big romantic hat covered with artificial roses and grapes and clouds of ostrich feathers.

More waves of sailors had arrived at The Tub of Diogenes. One was playing an accordion and another a saxophone, and women were dancing on the tables. Despite Emanuele's efforts, there were still many more sailors than women, and yet no one could put a hand out without touching a bosom or a thigh, which seemed to have got lost as it was impossible to tell who they belonged to; there were legs in mid-air and bosoms to be found knee-high. Velvety hands, creeping claws, sharply pointed red nails, quivering finger-ends, were groping at tunics, caressing muscles, tickling arms. And mouths met almost flying through the air, and stuck behind ears like clams, and huge lips seemed coated with scarlet almost up to the nostrils. Innumerable legs were squirming everywhere, like the tentacles of some enormous octopus, legs sliding about and colliding with haunches and thighs. And then everything seemed to melt away in the sailors' hands, and they found themselves holding a hat trimmed with bunches of grapes or a dental plate, or a stocking wrapped round the neck, or a sponge, or a piece of silk trimming.

Jolanda had remained alone in the little room with the giant sailor. The door was locked and she was combing her hair in front of the mirror over the wash-basin. The giant went to the window and pulled back the curtains. Outside could be seen the dark naval area and the mole with a line of lights reflected in the water. Then the giant began singing an American song which went: "The day is over, the night is falling, the skies are blue, the bells are beginning to ring."

And Jolanda approached the window too, and gazed out into the darkness, and their hands met on the window-sill and remained there motionless beside each other. And the big sailor went on singing in his voice of iron: "Children of God, let us sing Allelujah!"

And Jolanda repeated: "Let us sing Allelujah, Allelujah!"

During all this time Emanuele was anxiously moving round among the sailors without finding a sign of his wife, pushing away the bodies of excited women who every now and then fell into his arms. Suddenly, he was confronted by the group of taxi-drivers who had pushed in to get him to pay the fare shown on their meters. Emanuele's eyes were tearful, but they weren't going to let him go unless he paid. Now they were joined by old Baci, who was cracking his big coachman's whip and muttering: "If you don't pay up, I'll take her away again!"

Then whistles shrilled and the bar was surrounded by police. It was the patrol from the *Shenandoah* with rifles and helmets. They turned out all the sailors one by one. Then the Italian police trucks arrived, and loaded up all the women they could lay hands on.

The sailors were lined up outside the bar and marched off towards the port. The police trucks laden with women passed them on their way and there was a great shout of greetings from both sides. The giant sailor, who was in the leading file, began singing in his resounding voice: "The day is over, the sun is setting, let us sing Allelujah, Allelujah!"

Jolanda, squeezed inside a truck between Lollypop and the Wriggler, heard his voice getting farther away and took up the song: "The day is over, the work is done—Allelujah!"

And they all began singing the song, the sailors and the women, one lot going towards the port, the other towards the police station.

At The Tub of Diogenes Felice was beginning to pile up the tables. But Emanuele sat there slumped on a stool with his chin on his chest and his hat on the back of his head. They were just about to arrest him too, but the American officer in charge of the operations had made some inquiries and signed for him to be left alone. And now he, the officer, had also stayed on, and there were only the two of them left in the bar; Emanuele drooping desolately on his stool and the American standing in front of him with his arms crossed. When he was certain that they were quite alone, the officer shook the plump man by an arm and began talking to him. Felice approached to act as interpreter, a broad grin on his stubbly cobbler's face.

" Tell him that you can get him a girl too," he said to Emanuele.
Emanuele blinked his eyes, and then let his chin fall on his chest again.

" You to me, girl," said the officer. " Me to you, dollars."

" Dollars! . . ." Emanuele mopped his face with his handkerchief. He got up. " Dollars," he repeated. " Dollars."

He and the officer left the bar together. Night clouds were flying high in the sky. From the end of the mole the lighthouse was winking slowly, rhythmically. The air was still full of the song: " Allelujah!"

" The day is ending, the skies are blue, Allelujah!" sang Emanuele and the officer, as they strolled along in the middle of the street, arm-in-arm, in search of a haunt for an all-night spree.

Sleeping Like Dogs

EVERY TIME he opened his eyes he felt the acid yellow light of the big arc lamps in the ticket-hall glaring down at him; and he would pull up the lapels of his jacket in search of darkness and warmth. When he'd lain down he had not noticed how hard and icy the stone tiles on the floor were; now shafts of cold were coming up and infiltrating under his clothes and through the holes in his shoes, and the scarce flesh on his hips was aching, squashed between bone and stone.

But he'd chosen a good place, quiet and out of people's way, in that corner under the stairs; so much so that after he'd been there a little time four women's legs came high over his head and he heard voices say: "Hey, he's taken our place."

The man lying down heard, though he was not properly awake; a dribble was oozing from a corner of his mouth on to the bent cardboard of the little suitcase which was his pillow, and his hair had settled itself to sleep on its own following the horizontal line of his body.

"Well," said the same voice from above the dirty knees and the spreading bell of the skirt. "Let's put our things down. At least we can get our bed ready."

And one of those feet, a woman's in a boot, prodded his hips like a sniffling snout. The man pulled himself up on his elbows, blinking his stunned and aching pupils in the yellow light, while his hair was apparently taking no notice and standing up straight on its own. Then back he dropped as if he wanted to thump his head into the suitcase.

The women had taken the sacks off their heads. A man now came up behind, put down a roll of blankets and began to arrange them. "Hey," said the older of the women to the man lying down. "Move up, you, you can get underneath too, then." No answer; he was asleep.

"He must be dead tired," said the younger of the two women, who was all bones with the fleshy parts almost hanging as she bent down to spread the blankets and prop the sacks of flour underneath.

They were three black marketeers, on their way south with full sacks and empty tins; people whose bones had grown hard from sleeping on the floor in railway stations and travelling in cattle-trucks; but they had learnt to organise themselves and took blankets with them to put underneath for softness and above for warmth; the sacks and tins acted as pillows.

The older woman tried to slip a corner of blanket under the sleeping man, but had to raise him a bit at a time because he never moved. "He must really be dead tired," said the older woman. "Perhaps he's one of those emigrants."

Meanwhile the man with them, a thin man with zip-fasteners, had got between two of the blankets and pulled an end over his eyes. "Hey, come on underneath; aren't you ready?" he said to the back of the younger woman, who was still bending down arranging the sacks as pillows. She was his wife, the younger woman was, but they knew the floors of station waiting-rooms almost better than their marriage bed. The two women got underneath the blankets, and the younger one and her husband lay against each other making shivering noises, while the older one was tucking up that poor sleeping wretch. Perhaps the older one was not so old, but she was trodden down by the life she led, always lugging loads of flour and oil on her head up and down in those trains; her dress was like a sack itself and her hair went in all directions.

The head of the sleeping man was slipping off the suitcase, which was too high and ricked his neck; she tried to arrange him better, but his head nearly fell on the ground; so she propped his head on one of her shoulders and the man shut his lips, swallowed, settled further down on a softer part and began snoring again.

They were all just getting off to sleep, when a trio from Southern Italy arrived, a father with black moustaches and two dark plump daughters, all three very short; they were carrying wattle-baskets and their eyes were gummed with sleep under all that light. The daughters seemed to be wanting to go in one direction and he in another; so they were quarrelling, without looking each other in the face and almost without talking, except for short phrases between clenched teeth and jerky movements of the arms. When they found the place under the stairs already occupied by those four they stood there looking on more stunned than ever, until two youths in puttees with coats slung over their shoulders came up to them.

These two at once began trying to persuade the trio of Southerners to put all their blankets together and make up one group with the four already there. The two youths were Venetians emigrating to France, and they made the black market group get up and rearrange all the blankets so that the whole lot could settle down together. It was obvious that all this was just a manœuvre so as to be able to be next to the two girls, already half asleep; but finally they were all settled, including the older of the black-market women, who had not moved because she had that man's head sleeping on her breast. The two Venetians had, of course, got the girls in between them, leaving the father on one side; but their hands also succeeded in reaching the other women by groping about under the blankets and coats.

Someone was already snoring, but the father from Southern Italy could not manage to doze off in spite of all the sleep weighing on him. The acid yellow light burrowed right under his lids, under the hand covering his eyes; and the inhuman calls of the loud-speakers . . . " Slow train . . . platform . . . leaving . . ." kept him in a state of continual restlessness. He needed to urinate, too, but did not know where to go and was afraid of getting lost in that huge station. Finally he decided to wake one of the men and began shaking him; it was the unfortunate man who had been sleeping there first of all.

" The latrine, friend, the latrine . . ." he said, and pulled him by an elbow, sitting up in the middle of that heap of wrapped-up bodies.

The sleeping man suddenly sat up with a start and opened his misty red eyes and rubbery mouth on that face bending over him; a little wrinkled face, like a cat's, with black moustaches.

" The latrine, friend . . ." said the Southerner.

The other sat there stunned, glancing round in alarm. They both went on looking at each other open-mouthed, he and the man from Southern Italy. The man still half asleep could not understand anything; he found that woman's face on the floor beside him and gazed at it terror-struck. Perhaps he was just going to let out a shriek. Then suddenly he buried his head in the woman's breast again and dropped back into sleep.

The man from Southern Italy got up, overturning two or three bodies, and began moving with uncertain steps along that huge glaringly bright and cold hall. Through the windows could be seen the limpid darkness of the night and a view of geometric iron girders. He saw a dark little man even shorter than himself, in a flashy crumpled suit coming up to him with a careless air.

" The latrine, friend," the man from Southern Italy asked him imploringly.

" Cigarettes, American, Swiss," answered the other, who hadn't understood, showing the corner of a packet.

It was Belmoretto, who spent the whole year hanging round stations and had not a home or even a bed on the face of the earth, and who every now and again took a train and changed cities, wherever his uncertain trafficking in cigarettes and chewing-tobacco took him. At night he ended by joining up with some group sleeping in the station between trains, and so managed to lie down for an hour or two under a blanket; if not he wandered round till morning, unless he happened to run into someone who would take him home and give him a bath and some food and make him sleep with him. Belmoretto came from Southern Italy too; he was very kind to the old man with the black moustaches; he took him to the latrine and waited till he had finished, so as to accompany him back. He gave him a cigarette and they smoked together, looking through eyes sandy with sleep at the trains leaving and the mounds of people sleeping on the floor down in the hall below.

" We sleep like dogs," said the old man. " Six days and six nights since I've seen a bed."

" A bed," said Belmoretto. " Sometimes I dream of it, a bed. A lovely white bed all to myself."

The old man went back to try and get some sleep. He raised a blanket to make room for himself and saw the hand of one of the Venetians on the leg of one of his daughters. He tried to pull the hand away but the Venetian thought it was his friend trying to have a taste too, and pushed him. The old man cursed and raised his fist over him. The others shouted that they could not sleep and the old man eventually climbed back to his place on his knees and got under the blankets, quietly. He felt cold and curled himself up. A longing to cry came over him. Then, very cautiously, he advanced his hand among the nearest bodies and met two women's knees, which he began to stroke.

The older of the black-market women still had resting on her breast the face of the man who looked as if he had been squashed down by tons of sleep; wherever she touched him there was no reaction, only slight signs here and there of partial reawakening. Now the woman felt a hand, a small hand all lines and callouses, on her knee, and she squeezed her legs round the hand, which stopped and was quiet at once. The old man from Southern Italy could not manage to sleep but he felt happier; the soft warmth in which his little hand was wrapped seemed to be diffusing itself all over his body.

At that moment all of them felt a strange creature moving in among them, as if a dog were scooping among the blankets. One of the women screamed. The blankets were hurriedly pulled away so as to find out what it was. And in the middle of them they discovered Belmoretto, who was already snoring, his shoes off, and twisted up like a fœtus. He was woken by thumps on the back. " Excuse me," he said. " I didn't want to disturb you."

But now they were all awake and cursing, except for the first man, who was dribbling.

" One's bones are breaking, one's back's freezing," they were saying. " We ought to bust up that light and cut the line of that loud-speaker."

" I'll show you how to make up a mattress if you like," said Belmoretto.

" Mattress! " repeated the others. " Mattress! "

But Belmoretto had already cleared a bit of blanket and began to fold it up into pleats, in the way anyone who's been in prison knows. They told him to stop, as there weren't enough blankets and someone would find himself without any at all. Then they discussed how one couldn't sleep without something under one's head and not all of them had anything, as the Southerners' baskets weren't any use. Then Belmoretto arranged a complete system, by which every man rested his head on the leg of a woman; this was very difficult to do because of the blankets, but finally they were all arranged and a lot of new combinations resulted. But a little while later everything was in confusion again because they could not keep still; then Belmoretto managed to sell everyone a Nazionale cigarette and they all began to smoke and tell each other how many nights it was since they'd slept.

"Three weeks we've been travelling," said the Venetians. "Three times we've tried to pass this——frontier and they've turned us back. In France we'll get into the first bed we see and sleep for forty-eight hours on end."

"A bed," said Belmoretto. "With newly washed sheets and a feather mattress to sink into. A warm narrow bed, to be alone in."

"What about us, then, who've always led this life?" said the black-market man. "When we get home we spend a night in bed and then off we go on the trains again."

"A warm bed with clean sheets," said Belmoretto. "Naked, I'd get in, all naked."

"Six nights since we've taken our clothes off," said the old Southerner. "Since we've changed underclothes. Six nights we've been sleeping like dogs."

"I'd creep into a house like a thief," said one of the Venetians. "But not to steal. Just to get into a bed and sleep till morning."

"Or to steal a bed and bring it here to sleep in," said the other.

Belmoretto had an idea. "Wait," he said, and off he went.

He wandered round under the arches outside till he met Mad Maria. If Mad Maria spent a night without finding a client she had to go without a meal next day, so she never gave up even in the small hours and went on marching up and down those pavements till dawn, with her towlike red hair and her muscular calves. Belmoretto was a great friend of hers.

In the encampment at the station they were still talking about sleep and beds and the dogs' lives they led, and waiting for the darkness to clear in the windows. Ten minutes had not gone by when Belmoretto was back, with a rolled-up mattress on his shoulders.

"Down you get," he said, rolling it out on the floor. "Half an hour's turn for fifty *lire*; you can sleep two at a time. Down now, what's twenty-five *lire* a head?"

He had hired a mattress from Mad Maria, who had two on her

bed, and was now sub-letting it by the half-hour. Other sleepy travellers who were waiting to change trains came up, looking interested.

"Down you get," said Belmoretto. "I'll see about waking you. We'll put a blanket on top of you and then no one'll see you and you can do what you like. Down you get, now."

One of the Venetians tried first, together with one of the girls from Southern Italy. The older of the black-market women booked the second shift for herself and that poor sleeping man she was still propping up. Belmoretto had already pulled out a notebook and was jotting down the bookings, pleased as anything.

At dawn he'd take the mattress back to Mad Maria and they'd turn somersaults all over the bed till high noon. Then, finally, they'd fall asleep.

Desire in November

THE COLD hit the city one morning in November, under a deceitful sun in a clear calm sky; it cut like blades down the long straight streets, chasing the cats from the gutters back into kitchens with fires still unlit. People who had got up late and had not opened their windows went out in light overcoats saying once again, "Winter's late this year," then suddenly shivered as they breathed the icy air. But then they thought of the coal and wood supplies laid in during summer, and congratulated themselves on their own foresight.

It was a bad day for the poor, though; for now they had to face problems which they had so far put aside: heating, clothes. The public gardens were full of lanky youths eyeing the scraggy plane-trees and eluding the keepers, as they fingered the saws under their patched coats. A cluster of people was reading a notice about the distribution of winter vests and pants by a charitable organisation.

In one of the parishes the poor were told to collect these garments from a local priest, Don Grillo. Don Grillo lived in an old house with dark, narrow stairs, on to which the door of his flat opened directly over a slip of landing. Up these stairs the poor queued on distribution days, to knock one by one on the closed door, hand their certificates and coupons to an aged and lacrimose housekeeper, and then wait on the stairs again for her to return with the meagre bundle. Inside there was a glimpse of a room full of worm-eaten old furniture and of a table covered with bundles, at which sat Don Grillo, looking enormous and shouting in his deep resounding voice as he noted everything down in registers.

Sometimes the queue wound down past the corners of the stairs: widows in reduced circumstances who seldom left their attics, beggars with hacking coughs, dusty countrymen stamping about in hob-nailed boots, dishevelled youths—emigrants from somewhere or other—who wore sandals in winter and raincoats in summer. Sometimes this slow and squalid stream spread right on down past the mezzanine floor and the glass doors of Fabrizia, the furriers. And the elegant women going to Fabrizia to have their mink or astrakhan altered had to hug the banisters to avoid brushing against the ragged crew.

On the day that flannel vests and pants were being distributed at Don Grillo's, the queue was joined by a porter, a strong old man with a white beard streaked by locks of hair that were still blond. He was wearing a military overcoat and nothing underneath at all. Buttoned and muffled up though he was, his shins were bare and ended in a pair of boots without even any socks. People looked down and stood there open-mouthed; and he would laugh back. Under the fringe of white hair falling over his forehead he had two big, merry blue eyes, and a broad, vinous, happy face.

His name was Barbagallo and his clothes had been stolen from the river bank that summer while he was carrying loads of gravel. Till then he had got along with a few rags and a visit every now and then to prison or workhouse; but after a bit he was let out of prison and escaped from the workhouse, to wander round the city and the villages nearby, lazing about or doing an odd job as porter by the hour here and there. The fact that he had no clothes was a good excuse for begging or for getting put back in prison when he had nowhere better to go. The cold that morning had made him decide to lay hands on a suit, so he was going round naked except for that overcoat, terrifying the girls and being stopped by the police at every crossing as he was shuttled from one charity organisation to another.

On his joining the queue, no one spoke of anything else; meanwhile he was elbowing and pushing his way up the stairs, trying out every trick to get in front.

" Yes, yes, I'm naked! D'you see? Not just my legs! Would you like me to unbutton my coat? Hey, either you let me pass or I *will* unbutton! Am I cold? Never been better! Like to feel, madam, how warm I am? He's only handing out pants, the priest? What use are they to me? I'll take 'em, and then I'll go and sell 'em! "

Finally he sat down in the queue, on a step which was actually the landing in front of Fabrizia's. Ladies were coming and going, showing off their furs for the first time. " Oh," they cried, when they saw the bare legs of the old man sitting down outside.

" Now, don't call the police, madam, they've already had me up and sent me here to get myself some clothes. And anyway, I'm not showing anything, so don't make such a fuss."

The ladies passed hurriedly by, and Barbagallo felt himself brushed by the soft folds smelling of camphor and lily of the valley. " A fine fur, madame, unquestionably, it must be nice and warm under that! "

As each woman passed, he stretched out his hand and stroked her fur. " Help," they screamed. Then he rubbed his cheek against the furs like a cat.

There was a confabulation inside Fabrizia's; no one dared come out any more. " Should we call the police? " they asked each other. " But they've sent him here to get clothes! " Every now and then they opened the door a crack. " Is he still there? " Once he put his bearded head in through the door from where he was sitting. " Oooh! " They nearly fainted.

In the end Barbagallo made up his mind to go and parley with them. He got up and rang Fabrizia's bell. Two employees opened the door, one a pale woman who was all knees, and the other a girl with black plaits. "Call the ladies!" "Go away," said the pale woman. But Barbagallo did not let her shut the door. "Go and call 'em," he said to the other girl. She turned and went away. "Good girl," said Barbagallo. The owner of the shop appeared with her clients. "How much will you give me not to unbutton my coat?" said Barbagallo. "What?" "Come along, now, no nonsense!" And he began to unbutton himself from the neck with one hand, while holding the other out. The ladies hurriedly searched about in their bags for change to give him. One, a matron heavily loaded with jewels, did not seem to be able to find any change and was watching him from her big painted eyes. Barbagallo stopped unbuttoning. "Well, then; how much will you give me if I *do* unbutton?" "Hah, hah, hah!" exploded the shop girl with the plaits. "Linda!" shouted her mistress. Barbagallo pocketed the money and went out. "So long, Linda," he said.

In the queue the rumour was going round that there weren't enough clothes for everyone.

"Me first, as I'm naked!" exclaimed Barbagallo and succeeded in getting to the head.

The housekeeper at the door clasped her hands together at seeing him. "With nothing underneath! What's to be done! Wait, no, don't come in!"

"Let me pass, old girl, or I'll tempt you to sin. Where is His Reverence?"

And he went into the priest's room, among the sacred hearts bleeding away in their baroque frames, the towering cupboards and the crucifixes splayed all over the walls like black birds. Don Grillo rose from his desk and burst into a loud laugh:

"Ho, ho, ho! And who got you up like that? Ho, ho, ho!"

"Tell me, Father, to-day is the day for flannel underclothes, but I'm here for trousers. Have you any?"

The priest had flung himself back in his arm-chair with its high back and was laughing and laughing, his double chin and stomach in the air. "No, no, ho, ho, ho, no, I haven't any . . ."

"I'm not asking for a pair of yours, you know. . . . Well, in that case I'll have to stay here, till you telephone the Bishop and get me a pair sent over."

"That's it, that's it, my son, go to the Archbishop's, go to the palace, ho, ho, ho, I'll give you a note . . ."

"A note. And what about the flannel underclothes?"

And he began turning over sets of vests and long pants, but could not find a size large enough for Barbagallo. When they had found the biggest pair there was, Barbagallo said: "Now I'll put them on." The housekeeper was just in time to escape on to the landing before he took off his overcoat.

When he was naked, Barbagallo did a few exercises to warm himself up, then began to put on the underclothes. Don Grillo could not stop laughing at seeing that Garibaldi-like figure, squeezed from neck to wrists and down to the ankles into very tight vest and pants, with boots below.

"Eeeh!" cried Barbagallo, and sprang back as if he had had a shock.

"What's the matter, what's the matter, my son?"

"It tickles, it tickles me everywhere. . . . What's this vest you've given me, Father? I'm prickling all over!"

"Go on with you, it's new, you know, it's new, you'll soon get used to it."

"Oh, my skin's so delicate since I've got used to being naked. . . . Oooh, how it pricks me!" And he twisted himself round to scratch his back.

"Come on now, you've only to wash it once and it'll become as soft as silk . . . Now go to the address I've given you and they'll see about getting you a suit, off with you. . . ." And he pushed him towards the door, making him put on his overcoat again.

Barbagallo made no further resistance; he was a defeated man. They shut the door behind him. He began to go downstairs, doubled up, complaining and scratching himself, and all those still waiting in the queue asked him: " What've they done to you! Did they hit you? What a scandal! A priest, hitting a poor old man! What lovely pants, though," and they looked at his shins encased in white flannel.

Barbagallo seemed to have aged about ten years, his blue eyes were swollen with tears. He went on downstairs, and passed by the door of the furriers. Suddenly he turned round, stopped his complaining, and knocked.

The shop-girl with the plaits peeped out from the door. " But . . ." she said. " Look," said Barbagallo with a smile on his still tearful face, and pointed to the white pants on his ankles. And the girl exclaimed: " Oh . . ."

He was inside now. " Call your mistress, go on! " The girl went out. Barbagallo leapt into a side room and locked himself in. The Signora Fabrizia came, did not see him and went back shaking her head. " Why they don't keep madmen shut up, I don't know. . . ."

As soon as the key had turned in the lock, Barbagallo tore off his overcoat, the vest, the boots, and the pants, and breathed freely, naked at last. He saw himself reflected in a large mirror, flexed his muscles, and did some exercises. There was no heating and it was bitterly cold, but he felt very happy. Then he began to look around.

He had locked himself into Fabrizia's store-room. Hung on a long clothes-stand were all the furs in a row. The old man's eyes shone with joy. Furs! He began to pass his hands along them from one to the other, as if playing a harp; then he rubbed his shoulder, his face in them. There was grey and sullen mink, astrakhan of voluptuous softness, silver foxes like grassy clouds, grey squirrels and stone martens exquisitely smooth and light, firm brown, cosy beavers, good-natured and dignified rabbits, little white speckled goats with a dry rustle, leopards with a shuddering caress. Barbagallo noticed that his teeth were chattering from the cold. He took a lambswool jacket and tried it on; it fitted him like a glove. He tied a fox fur round his hips, twisting the tawny tail to make a loincloth. Then he slipped into a sable coat which must have been made for an enormous woman, it wrapped him round with such big, soft folds. He also found a pair of boots lined with beaver, and then a beautiful bearskin hat: he really was comfortable. A muff, and he was set. He preened himself in front of the mirror for a bit; it was impossible to distinguish what was beard and what was fur.

The clothes-stand was still loaded with furs. Barbagallo flung them to the ground, one by one, until he had a wide soft bed under him to sink into. Then he stretched out and made all the rest of the furs cascade down on top of him like an avalanche. It was so warm that it seemed a pity to fall asleep and not enjoy just lying there, but the old porter could not hold out for long and soon sank into a serene and dreamless sleep.

He woke up and saw night through the window. All around, silence. Obviously the fur shop was shut and he wondered how he would ever get out. He listened, and thought he heard a cough in the adjoining room. A light filtered through the keyhole.

He got up, decked with mink, silver foxes, antelopes and bearskin hat, and slowly opened the door. The girl with the black plaits was sewing bent over a table, by the light of a lamp. Owing to the value of the goods in the store-room, the Signora Fabrizia made one of the girls stay and sleep in a bed in the work-room, to give the alarm in case of theft.

"Linda," said Barbagallo. The girl opened her eyes wide and there, standing in the shadow, saw a gigantic human bear with its arms entwined in an astrakhan muff. "How lovely . . ." she said.

Barbagallo took a few steps up and down, peacocking like a model.

Linda said: "But now I must call the police."

"The police!" Barbagallo was upset. "But I'm not stealing

anything. What can I do with these things? Obviously I can't go round the streets like this. I only came in here to take off my vest which was prickling me."

They arranged that he would stay the night there and leave early in the morning. And what was more, Linda knew how to wash flannel so that it would not tickle him any more, and would wash his vest and pants for him.

Barbagallo helped her to wring them out and put up the line, then hang them near the electric fire. Linda had some apples, which they ate.

Barbagallo then said: "Let's see how you look in these furs." And he made her try them all on, in all variations, with her plaits up and with her hair loose, and they exchanged impressions on the softness of the various furs against the skin.

Finally, they constructed a hut entirely of furs, big enough for them both to lie under, and they went inside to sleep.

When Linda awoke he was already up and putting on the vest and pants. The dawn was showing through the window.

"Are they quite dry?"

"A little damp, but I must go."

"Do they still tickle?"

"Not a bit, I'm as comfortable as a Pope."

He helped Linda tidy up the store-room, put on his military overcoat, and said good-bye to her at the door.

Linda stood watching him as he walked away, with the white strip of pants between his overcoat and boots, and the proud tuft of hair in the cold dawn air.

Barbagallo had no intention of asking for a suit at the Archbishop's palace; he had got a new idea—going round the squares of the surrounding villages in his vest and pants, giving exhibitions of physical strength.

A Judgement

THAT MORNING Judge Onofrio Clerici noticed something different about the way people were going about the streets. Every day he drove across the city in a narrow carriage, from his home to the Courts of Justice; and below him as he went the pavements were always crammed with squalid crowds, jostling each other with dirty hunched shoulders, blocking the pavements round the stalls of roasted meat, while blind men shouted: " Lottery . . . millions . . ." and exercise-books thumped dully in the satchels of children going to school, and snails jutted out of baskets of vegetables and red celery.

But there was something changed, something new stirring in this mob now; whites of eyes were showing in cold triangles from slanting lids, and teeth between lips; coats and shawls seemed to be falling more crisply over the hunched shoulders, chins jutting sharply above jerseys and coat-lapels; and Judge Onofrio Clerici felt a growing sense of discomfort.

For weeks now the chalk scrawls on the walls of his home had been growing both in number and size; scrawls of gallows and of men hanging on them, men who always wore a judge's high tubular cap with a round tassel on its flat top. For a long time Judge Onofrio Clerici had realised that the people hated him and muttered complaints in court against his sentences, and that when the widows of partisans gave witness they were crying out more against him than at the men in the dock; but he was quite certain of himself and of his actions, and he hated them too, this filthy populace who could not give their evidence clearly, or even sit respectfully on the public benches, this populace which was always loaded with children and debts and twisted ideas; the populace of Italy.

Yes, some time ago Judge Onofrio Clerici had realised what most Italians are like; women always pregnant carrying scrofulous babies, blue-cheeked youths who, if it wasn't for the war, would be good for nothing but unemployment and selling tobacco at railway stations; old men with asthma and ruptures and hands so full of callouses they couldn't even hold a pen to sign their statements; a discontented, whining, quarrelsome lot, who'd take everything they could get if they weren't controlled, would install themselves everywhere, dragging their scrofulous urchins and their ruptures with them, trampling the remains of their roasted meat into the pavements.

Luckily, though, there were the decent people too, the people with smooth flabby skins, hairs in their noses and ears, and rumps as stable as foundation stones in their upholstered arm-chairs, people tinkling with honours and decorations, necklaces, dangling spectacles, eyeglasses, hearing aids, dental plates; people who had sat throughout the centuries on the baroque arm-chairs of the chancellories of old kingdoms; people who know how to make laws and apply them and get them respected in a way useful to themselves; people linked together by a secret understanding, a common discovery that most Italians are a filthy lot and that it would be better for Italy if they had never existed or at least did not make themselves so much heard.

Judge Onofrio Clerici arrived at the Courts of Justice, an old building still half in ruins from past bombings, propped by rotting beams, with plaster flaking and baroque coats-of-arms crumbling on the façade. As always at trials, a mob was jostling round the closed doors, held back by police. It had become a custom to reserve the public benches for friends and relations of the accused and for persons who were trustworthy and respectable; and yet each time some of the mob managed to worm their way into the court-room and find places on the benches at the back, from which they disturbed the sittings with their protests and hisses. The rest of them stayed outside, rioting, shouting threats, waving placards; the uproar would reach the court-room in gusts, ruffling the nerves of Judge Onofrio Clerici and confirming his loathing for these petulant Italians, who were for ever complaining and making nuisances of themselves about things they did not understand.

That day, though, the crowd was unusually silent and composed, and there was not the usual hostile mutter at seeing Judge Onofrio Clerici alight from his ramshackle carriage and enter the Courts of Justice by a side door.

Inside the Courts of Justice the sense of discomfort in the judge's heart calmed down a little; everyone in there were personal friends, judges and public prosecutors and lawyers, all decent people, with smiles buried at the corners of their lips and throats throbbing like frogs' gills. They felt calm and smug now, these people did: in the government and all the high offices of state there were others like them, with drooping eyelids and throbbing throats, and gradually those other Italians would be put back in their places and become resigned to the sores and ruptures they had put up with now for centuries.

While they were waiting for the beginning of the audience, and the officials of the court were wrapping themselves in their black robes, a lawyer with a face covered with warts had taken from his pocket a newspaper full of articles against the other Italians, and, laughing loudly, was showing his colleagues some grotesque drawings in which three Italians were shown as clumsy monsters wearing peaked caps and carrying ridiculous cudgels. The only one who did not laugh at the drawings was the new Clerk of the Court, an old man with a long head and a mild, respectful air; one by one the magistrates glanced from laughter-congested eyes at his sad, lined face and the laughter died away in their frog-like throats. " That man isn't to be trusted," thought Judge Onofrio Clerici.

Then the court opened for the trial. The trials which Judge Onofrio Clerici was presiding over at that time were not the usual ones against a few starving wretches for house-breaking. They were trials of people who had had Italians arrested and shot during a recent war, and as Judge Onofrio Clerici listened to their defences, he had become convinced that they were respectable people who followed their own ideas, the sort of people who were still needed to keep in order those other Italians who were always so haggard and filthy, always starving, always whining about something new.

But Judge Onofrio Clerici held the reins of the laws in his hands, and the laws had always been made by his own people, the ones with the frog-like throats, even when they seemed made on behalf of those other poor devils: he knew that laws can be turned round in any direction and black made to say white and white black. So he freed all the accused, and after the trials the crowds stayed out in the squares till late at night and women in mourning screamed and wept for their men-folk who had been hanged.

As he took his place on his throne Judge Onofrio Clerici scrutinised the public; they all seemed trustworthy people; men with long jutting teeth and eyebrows down on their noses like birds of prey; and ladies with bony yellow necks wearing hats decorated with veils. But when he looked beyond them the judge noticed that the whole of the last line of benches was occupied by a squalid lot who had pushed their way inside in spite of orders; pale girls with plaits, cripples with chins propped on crutches, young men with blue eyes buried in wrinkles, old men with spectacles mended with string, old women wrapped to the eyes in shawls. This last line of benches was a little apart from the ones in front, and those intruders were sitting there motionless with arms folded, all looking straight at him, the judge.

That feeling of discomfort tightened round the heart of Judge Onofrio Clerici. Two policemen were standing each side of the magistrate's rostrum, put there no doubt to protect him from any possible protests by those desperadoes; but their faces looked different from the usual police, they were pale and sad, with tufts of fair hair sprouting from the sides of their caps. And then that Clerk of the Court was continually bent over his table and seemed to be writing something all on his own.

The accused man was already sitting impassively in the dock, wearing a clean well-pressed suit. He had dark grey, carefully combed hair growing low over his eyes and temples, and very light pupils which seemed lost in the reddish surrounds of eyes without lashes or eyebrows; his lips were thick, but of the same colour as his skin, and when he opened them he showed big square teeth. The beard under his shaven skin left a shadow like marble. His hands, which were grasping the bars with a calm gesture, had big flat fingers like rubber stamps.

The case began. The witnesses were the usual whining filthy lot: they shouted, particularly the women, waving their arms at the dock. "It's him . . . I saw it with my own eyes . . . him who said ' Now you'll pay for it, you bandits ' . . . my only child, my Gianni . . . that's what he said; ' You won't talk ? All right then, you swine . . . ' "

"These people don't know how to give evidence properly," thought Judge Onofrio Clerici, " they're confused, undisciplined and disrespectful; " after all that man in the dock had been one of their superiors and they had disobeyed them. And now the man in the dock was giving them a lesson in behaviour, sitting there impassively, looking at them through those colourless pupils, without denying anything, looking slightly bored.

Judge Onofrio Clerici envied his calm. That sense of discomfort was still growing, he found. And a hammering outside in the courtyard was getting on his nerves. They must be working to prop up the ever-shaky building; through the high, rather

137

ecclesiastical windows of the court-room he could see poles and planks being carried about in bare arms. "I wonder why they're working while there's a case being heard?" Judge Onofrio Clerici asked himself, and was on the point, once or twice, of sending the usher to tell them to stop, but something held him back every time. Now a reconstruction was being made through witnesses of the chief crime against the accused: the slaughter of men, women and old folk on the square of a village which had then been set on fire. Gradually Judge Onofrio Clerici built up a clear vision of the pile of corpses in the middle of the square; and he interrogated the witnesses with the most meticulous care to reconstruct the scene in its minutest detail. The bodies had been left in the square for a day and a night, without anyone being allowed to go near them; Onofrio Clerici thought of those yellow bony bodies in their blood-clotted rags, with blue-bottles settling on the lips and nostrils. The public in the last row was still quiet, for some reason: and to overcome the feeling of disturbance they made him feel, Judge Onofrio Clerici tried to imagine them, too, as piled-up corpses with eyes open like holes and trickles of blood under their nostrils.

"Then he went up to our dead," one of the witnesses, a bent old man with a beard, was saying. "I watched him; and he stopped in front of them; and this is what he did to our dead; why, it'd disgust me to do it to him; he spat at them."

Judge Onofrio Clerici saw those corpses lying there, already yellow, with bony legs, and felt the saliva rising to his lips too. He looked at the thick pale lips of the accused, and felt a secret urge to see the saliva coming from those lips. And at the memory the accused man opened his lips and there above the big square teeth appeared a slight froth; oh, how Judge Onofrio Clerici understood the accused man's disgust, the revulsion which had made him spit on those dead bodies.

Now the Counsel for the Defence was making his final speech; he was the paunchy little man with a face covered in warts who had been so amused by those caricatures against the poor. He praised the merits of the accused, his activities as a zealous public servant, all dedicated to the preservation of order; and he asked, in consideration of the extenuating circumstances, for the minimum sentence.

During this speech Judge Onofrio Clerici did not know where to look. If he let his eyes rest on the public benches he was at once disturbed by the gaze of those people at the back, those eyes interminably looking straight at him. And outside that hammering and dragging about of planks never seemed to stop. . . . Now, on the other side of the window had appeared a rope, and two hands unrolling it, as if to see how long it was. What on earth was it for, that rope?

The Public Prosecutor was talking now. He was a man with long bones, leaning on jutting hips, and he mouthed his words through carmine gums crossed by veils of spittle. He began by talking about the need to bring before the courts the many crimes committed at that period, and to punish the real culprits; then he added that the accused was certainly not one of those and that he could not have avoided doing what he had done. He ended by requesting half the sentence asked for by the Counsel for the Defence.

The public in the front rows applauded, with a strange sound of bones rattling together as they clapped. Judge Onofrio Clerici thought; now those at the back will begin shouting, but they remained motionless and intent, why he couldn't understand.

The magistrates retired to deliberate in an adjoining room. From a window in this room there was a clear view of the court-yard and finally Judge Onofrio Clerici was able to understand what the workmen were doing outside there with those poles and that rope. A gallows; they had built a gallows right in the middle of the courtyard; it was finished now and there it stood, bare and black with the noose dangling down; the workmen had gone.

"Ignorant fools," thought Judge Onofrio Clerici. "They

think the accused will be condemned to death, so they've built a gallows. But I'll just show them!" And to teach them a lesson he proposed to the other magistrates, by means of legal quibbles which only he knew, that the accused be absolved. The magistrates unanimously approved his proposal.

When the sentence was read out it was the judge who seemed the person most moved. No one blinked an eye, neither the accused with his flat fingers round the bars, nor the decent public, nor the intruders. The pale girls in plaits, the cripples, the old women in shawls, were all standing up, their heads high, glaring at him.

The Clerk of the Court approached with the documents of the case for the judge to sign: from the humble sadness with which he submitted the sheets, he might have been bringing a death sentence. Sheets; for under the first one there was another of which the Clerk of the Court only uncovered the bottom corner by slipping the top one up slightly. And the judge signed that too, under the glare from those benches of the spectacles tied with string and of the wrinkled blue eyes. The judge was sweating.

And now, suddenly the Clerk of the Court slipped the top sheet off completely: and there, on the sheet underneath Judge Onofrio Clerici read: "Onofrio Clerici, judge, guilty of having for a long time insulted and derided us other poor Italians, is condemned to die like a dog." And beneath this was his signature.

The two police with the sand blond faces had moved up beside him. But they did not touch him.

"Judge Onofrio Clerici," they said. "Come with us."

Judge Onofrio Clerici turned. The policemen, one on each side, still without touching him, led him through a little door into the deserted courtyard to the foot of the gallows.

"Get up on to that gallows," they said.

But they did not push him. "Get up," they said. Onofrio Clerici got up.

"Put your head in the noose," they said.

The judge thrust his head into the slip-knot. The two below scarcely looked at him.

"Now, give the stool a kick," they said, and went away.

Judge Onofrio Clerici kicked away the stool and felt the rope tighten round his neck, his throat shut up like a fist, his bones wrench apart. And his eyes strained out of their sockets like big black snails as if the light they were looking for could be converted into air. Meanwhile the darkness was growing thicker in the arcades of the deserted courtyard; deserted because those filthy Italians had not even come to see him die.

The Cat and the Policeman

A SEARCH for hidden arms had begun in the city some time ago. The police would climb up on the open trucks, their leather helmets making all their faces look inhuman and alike, and set off. with sirens sounding, for the poor quarters, to turn out the cupboards and unscrew the stove-pipes in some worker's home. During those days a policeman called Bavarino found himself in the grip of a gnawing anxiety.

Bavarino had been unemployed until joining the police force a short time before. So it was only quite recently that he had been told of a secret deep in the heart of this apparently calm and hard-working city; behind the concrete walls lining the streets, in hidden enclosures and dark corners, were, it was said, whole forests of gleaming fire-arms, waiting threateningly like the prickles of a porcupine. There was talk of piles of machine-guns, underground dumps of bullets, even of a complete field-gun hidden in a room behind a walled-up door. Pistols were said to have been found sewn into mattresses in the workers' homes and rifles nailed under floorboards, like metal filings indicating the presence of a nearby mine-field. Bavarino felt ill at ease among his own people; every hole, every pile of rubbish seemed strange and menacing; he often thought of that hidden field-gun, and sometimes found himself imagining it in the parlour of a home in his childhood, one of those rooms which remain closed for years at a time. He saw the gun lying between the faded lace-bordered velvet sofas, its muddy wheels on the carpet and the gun-carriage touching the chandelier; huge, filling the whole room, and scratching the polish off the piano.

One evening the police made a raid on the working-class quarter and cordoned off an entire tenement. It was a large block with a tired, shabby air about it, as if supporting so much hedged-in humanity had deformed the walls and floors, turned them into porous, calloused flesh.

The courtyard was cluttered with barrels of refuse, and round each floor ran railings and landings of twisted rusty iron, the railings with clothes and rags draped all over them, the landings with windows covered in bits of wood through which stuck the blackened pipes of stoves; at the end of each landing, one above the other like turrets in a ruined castle, were lavatory huts, interspersed from floor to floor by little windows clattering with sewing-machines and smoky with cooking, right on up to the battered skylights, the crooked gutters and the filthy attics.

Criss-crossing up from the basement to the roof of the old building ran a labyrinth of foul stairs, like black veins, along which were scattered apparently haphazard the entrance doors to mezzanine floors and flats.

The police climbed up, their steps echoing lugubriously, trying to make out the names written on the doors; round and round the reverberating landings they went in single file, amid the peering heads of children and tousled women

Bavarino was in the middle of them, indistinguishable from the rest in his automaton's helmet, which threw a sharp shadow over his cloudy blue eyes; but his heart was a prey to confusing and disturbing thoughts. Their enemies, he'd been told, the enemies of the police and decent people, were hidden away inside this building. Bavarino looked anxiously at the half-closed doors of the rooms; in every chest of drawers, behind every cupboard, terrible weapons might be hidden. Why did every tenant, every woman there, look at them distrustfully and anxiously? If among

them was an enemy, mightn't they all be enemies too? Behind
the walls on the stairs, refuse could be heard falling with heavy
thuds down the chutes; mightn't that be weapons being hastily
got rid of?

They went into a low room; a family was having supper round
a plank covered with a red and white check cloth. The children
were crying. Only the smallest, eating on its father's knee, looked
at them silently, with black, hostile eyes. " Orders to search the
house," said the sergeant, with a sketchy salute which made the
coloured cordons on his chest bounce. " *Madonna!* Us poor folk!
Who've been honest all our lives!" said an old woman with a
hand on her heart. The father was in his vest and had a broad
open face and a stubbly beard; he was feeding the child with a
spoon. He glanced at them sideways, perhaps ironically at
first; then he shrugged his shoulders and turned back to the
child.

The room was so full of policemen that it was impossible to
turn round. The sergeant gave out useless orders and hampered
rather than directed the operations. Anxiously Bavarino inspected
every piece of furniture, every cupboard. That man in the vest,
there, he was an enemy! And anyway, even if he had not been
one till this moment, he must certainly become one now on
seeing drawers being turned upside down and pictures of the
Madonna and his dead parents torn from the walls. And if he was
their enemy, why then this place must be full of traps: every
drawer might contain carefully dismembered machine-guns; and
if he opened the dresser he might find bayonets fixed on rifles
pointing at his chest; perhaps under the jackets hanging on pegs
dangled belts of shiny bullets; every saucepan, every pot might
hide a hand grenade.

Bavarino moved his long thin arms about uncomfortably.
There was a tinkle from a drawer; daggers? No, spoons and
forks. Some papers gave out a hollow thud; bombs? No, books.
The bedroom was so full it was impossible to cross it; there were

two double beds, three camp-beds, and two mattresses on the floor. And at the other end of the room, sitting in a cot, was a baby crying with toothache. Bavarino would have liked to push open a gap between those beds to make sure there was nothing there; but supposing he found himself standing over a hidden arsenal, supposing every bed concealed a mortar?

Round and round Bavarino went, without getting anything searched. He tried to open a door; it resisted. The field-gun, perhaps! He thought of it in that parlour of his childhood, with a vase of artificial flowers sprouting out from the barrel and little china figures perched innocently on the mounts. Suddenly the door gave way; it was not a parlour but a storing place, with broken straw chairs and boxes. Dynamite? There, on the floor, Bavarino saw the marks of two wheels; something on wheels had been dragged out of this place by way of a narrow passage. Bavarino followed the tracks. It was the grandfather pushing the pram away as quickly as he could. Why was that old man running away? Perhaps that blanket over his legs was hiding a hatchet! If I pass near him the old man will split my head in two! But he was only going to the lavatory. Was the secret there, perhaps? Bavarino ran along the landing, but the lavatory door opened and a little girl with a red bow came out carrying a cat.

Bavarino thought he might make friends with the children, then question them. He put out a hand to stroke the cat. " Nice pussy," he said. The cat jumped away, nearly bumping into him; it was a thin, stringy, grey cat with a mangy coat. It was baring its teeth and leaping about like a dog. " Nice pussy," said Bavarino, trying to stroke it, as if his only problem was to make friends with this cat. But the cat gave a sideways skip and ran off, turning every now and then to give him a malevolent look.

Bavarino went running after it down the landing, calling out, " Nice pussy, nice pussy." He got into a room where two girls were working away, bent over sewing-machines. The floor was covered with piles of snippings. " Firearms?" asked the policeman and scattered the material with his foot, which got entangled with little bits of pink and mauve stuff. The girls laughed.

He turned a corner and ran up a flight of stairs; sometimes the cat seemed to be waiting for him, then when he got nearer it jumped away on outstretched paws. He came out on another landing: it was blocked by a bicycle with its wheels in the air: a little man in overalls was dipping a tyre into a can of water and looking for a puncture. The cat had already hopped to the other side. "Excuse me," said the policeman. "There it is," said the little man, asking him to look; from the inner tube in the water rose thousands of tiny bubbles. "Excuse me." Has all this been purposely put there to block his way, or to make him fall over the railings?

He passed on. In one room there was only a bed on which a young man with a bare chest lay on his back smoking, his hands clasped behind his curly head. This looked suspicious. "Excuse me, but have you seen a cat?" That was a good excuse to search under the bed. Bavarino stretched a hand out underneath, and was immediately pecked. Out jumped a chicken, kept secretly at home in spite of the local laws. The bare-chested young man did not bat an eyelid; he just went on lying there, smoking.

Across a landing the policeman found himself in the workroom of a bespectacled man making hats. "Search . . . orders . . ." said Bavarino, and a pile of hats, soft felts, straws and velours, fell and scattered all over the floor. Suddenly the cat jumped out from behind a curtain, played with the hats for a quick second, then whisked off. Bavarino no longer knew whether he wanted to make friends with it or not.

In the middle of a kitchen sat an old man in a postman's cap; his trousers were rolled up and he was bathing his feet. As soon as he saw the policeman he grinned and pointed towards an inner room. Bavarino peered in. "Help," screamed a fat woman who was almost naked. Embarrassed, Bavarino muttered excuses. The postman grinned, his hands on his knees. Bavarino crossed the kitchen again and went out on to a terrace.

The terrace was entirely draped with clothes hanging out to dry. The policeman groped his way through blind white corridors, a labyrinth of sheets; every now and then the cat reappeared, sliding from under the corner of a sheet, then squatting down and vanishing under another. Suddenly Bavarino felt frightened he'd got lost; perhaps he was shut outside there, his fellow-policemen had already left the building, and he was a prisoner of these people who were quite rightly offended with him, a prisoner among these white sheets. He found a gap, finally, and was able to peer over a low wall. Below opened the well of the courtyard, with lights beginning to go on round the landing. And Bavarino did not know whether it was with fear or relief that he saw policemen swarming like ants along the railings and up and down the stairs, and heard shouts of orders and cries of protests and alarm.

The cat was sitting on the wall beside him, moving its tail and looking about it with an air of indifference. But whenever he moved it jumped away, then vanished up a narrow staircase leading to an attic. The policeman followed; he no longer felt frightened. The attic was almost empty. Outside the moon had begun to glimmer on the black buildings. Bavarino took off his helmet; his face became human again, a thin blond boy's face.

" Not a step farther," said a voice. " I've got you covered."

On the step by the big window was crouching a girl with long hair down to her shoulders, painted lips, silk stockings and no shoes. She was reading out loud with a snivelling voice in the fading light from a picture paper covered in drawings and a few phrases in block letters.

" Gun? " asked Bavarino, and took her by a wrist to open her hand. As soon as she moved her arm the cardigan opened at her breast, and the cat, rolled up into a ball, jumped out at the police-man, baring its teeth. But now Bavarino realised it was just a game.

Away over the tiles rushed the cat and Bavarino, leaning over the low rail, watched it as it ran off safe and free among the rooftops.

"And by her bed Mary saw the baronet in evening dress," the girl went on reading, "pointing a gun at her."

All around the lights were going on in the workers' homes, high and lonely as towers. Bavarino saw the vast city stretching out below him; symmetrical constructions of iron and concrete loomed inside the factory boundaries, and wisps of smoke from the tops of chimney stacks floated across the sky.

"Do you want my pearls, Sir Henry?" persisted that nasal voice. "No, I want you, Mary."

As the wind blew up, Bavarino felt that intricate mass of iron and concrete was against him; the porcupine was raising its spikes from a thousand hiding-places. And now he was alone in enemy territory.

"I have riches and wealth, I live in a sumptuous palace, I have servants and jewels, what more can I ask of life?" went on the girl, her black hair falling over the pages scattered with slinking women and men with flashing smiles.

Bavarino heard the shrill cry of whistles and the rumble of engines; the police were leaving the building. He would have liked to fly away under the chain of clouds in the sky, and bury his pistol in a big hole scooped out of the ground.

Who Put the Mine in the Sea?

AT THE villa of Pomponio the financier, the guests were taking coffee on the veranda. There was General Amalasunta, who was explaining the third world war with cups and spoons, and the Signora Pomponio smiling and saying: "How ghastly," like the cool-headed woman she was.

Only the Signora Amalasunta allowed herself to show any alarm, but this was permissible in her case, with her husband courageously proposing immediate total war on all four fronts. "Let's hope it won't last long," she said.

Strabonio, the journalist, was sceptical. "Oh, well, everything's been foreseen," he said. "You remember, sir, that in my article even a year ago . . ."

"Yes, yes," yawned Pomponio, who remembered the article well, as Strabonio had written it after an interview with him.

"However, one must not exclude . . ." said Senator Uccellini, who had just failed to give a very clear picture of the pacific mission of the Papacy, before, during and after the inevitable conflict.

"Of course, yes of course . . ." the others rejoined in conciliatory tones. The Senator's wife was Pomponio's mistress, and they felt he had to be humoured.

Through the gaps in the striped awning the sea could be seen rubbing itself against the beach like a tranquil, abstracted cat, arching its back to the passing breeze.

A servant entered and asked them if they wanted any sea urchins or cockles. An old man had arrived with two baskets full of them. The discussion on the dangers of war quickly passed to the dangers of typhus; the general quoted episodes in Africa, Strabonio cited literary incidents, and the senator agreed with everyone. Pomponio, who was something of an expert, said he would choose himself, and ordered the old man to be brought in with his baskets.

The old man was called Baci of the Rocks. He made some fuss with the servant as he didn't want anyone else to touch his baskets. There were two of them, both half-broken and mouldy; one he had on his hip and let fall to the ground as soon as he came in; the other he carried on his shoulder—it must have been very heavy, for he was bent under the weight and lowered it very gently to the ground. Round the top was tied a piece of old sacking.

The whole of Baci's head was covered by white down, with no space between hair and beard. The small patches of skin that did show were bright red, as if the sun over the years had succeeded only in boiling and scorching rather than tanning it; and his eyes were bloodshot as if even the moisture in them had been transformed into salt. He had a short, boyish body with knobbly limbs jutting through the rents in his ancient suit, worn next to the skin, without even a shirt. His shoes, too, must have been fished from the sea, they were so deformed and parchment-like, and didn't even match. His whole body emanated a pungent smell of rotting seaweed. "How picturesque," the ladies all commented.

Baci of the Rocks uncovered the lighter basket, and went round showing a heap of shiny black sea-urchins with prickles still grinding. He handled them with his two wizened hands as if they were rabbits to be taken by the ears, turning them over to display the soft red flesh. Under the sea urchins was a layer of sacking, and under that the cockles, their bearded mossy shells covering flat yellow and brown striped flesh.

Pomponio examined and sniffed them all carefully. "They're not grown in the drains in your parts by any chance, are they?" he asked.

Baci smiled into his beard. "Oh, no, I'm on the headland, the drains are here, where you bathe . . ."

The guests quickly changed the subject. They bought some sea-urchins and cockles and asked Baci to bring them more in the next few days. They even gave him their visiting cards so that he could call round at their villas.

"And what have you got in the other basket?" they asked.

"Ah," said the old man with a wink, "a very big fish. One I'm not selling."

"And what are you going to do with it then? Eat it yourself?"

"Eat it! It's a fish made of iron . . . I must find its owner to return it. Then he can take care of it himself, can't he?"

The others did not understand.

"You see," he explained, "I always sort out the things washed up by the sea. Tins on one side, shoes on another and bones on another still. And now this thing comes along. What'll I do with it? I saw it out at sea, half on top and half under the water, rusty and green with seaweed. Why they put these things in the sea I can't understand. Would you like to find it under your bed? Or in your cupboard? I fished it out and now I'm trying to find who put it in, and I'll tell him, 'There, you can look after it a bit now!'"

As he was talking he went up to the basket, undid the sacking on top, and revealed a big, monstrous iron object. The ladies did not understand what it was at first, but when General Amalasunta exclaimed "It's a mine!" they screamed and the Signora Pomponio fainted.

There was general confusion, one trying to fan the Signora, another reassuring everyone: "It's quite harmless, of course, after so many years in the sea"; another saying: "It must be taken

151

away at once, and that old man arrested." But the old man had vanished, both he and his terrible basket.

The host called the servants. "Have you see him? Where's he gone to?" No one could assure him that he had really left. "Search the whole house; open up all the cupboards, all the drawers, empty out the cellar!"

"Every man for himself!" cried Amalasunta suddenly turning pale. "This house is in danger—out of it everyone!"

"But why only my house?" protested Pomponio. "What about yours, General?"

"I must go and look after my place," said Strabonio, remembering certain prized possessions.

"Pietro!" cried the Signora Pomponio, coming to and throwing herself on her husband's neck.

"Pierino!" cried the Signora Uccellini, also throwing herself on Pomponio's neck and encountering his legitimate spouse.

"Luisa!" observed Senator Uccellini. "Let us go home!"

"You don't imagine your house is any safer?" they said to him. "What with the policy your party's following, you're in more danger than any of us!"

Then Uccellini had a flash of genius. "Let's call the police!"

The police were loosed all over the seaside town to search for the old man with his mine. The villas of Pomponio, General Amalasunta, Strabonio, Senator Uccellini and others were picketed with armed guards and searched from cellar to ceiling by Army Engineer units with mine-detectors.

That night all the people who had been at the Villa Pomponio camped out in the open.

Meanwhile a smuggler called Grimpante, who always managed to get to know everything through his contacts, set out on his own to find old Baci. Grimpante was a big, gross man who wore a sailor's white drill cap; the shadier deals on both sea and shore all passed through his hands. Grimpante was soon making a tour

of the taverns in the Old Quarter and before long ran into Baci
coming out of one, drunk, with the mysterious basket on his
shoulder.

He invited him for a glass at the Tavern of the Earless Man,
and as he poured out the drink began to explain his plan.

"It's useless trying to return the mine to its owner," he said,
"he'll only put it back where you found it as soon as he can.
Instead, if you listen to me, we can catch enough fish to swamp
all the markets along the coast and make ourselves millionaires in
a few days."

Now there was a certain urchin called Zefferino who always
poked his nose into everything, and had followed the pair into
the Tavern of the Earless Man and hidden under the table. He soon
realised what Grimpante meant, and ran off to spread the news
among all the poor in the Old Quarter.

"Hey, do you want some fish to fry to-day?"

From the narrow, crooked windows leant out thin, dishevelled
women with babies at the breast, old folk with ear trumpets,
housewives cleaning vegetables, and unemployed youths in the
middle of shaving.

"What's that, what's that?"

"Sssh, sssh, come along with me," said Zefferino.

Grimpante called in at his home, picked up an old violin-case
and set off with Baci. They took the road running along the sea.
Behind them on tiptoe followed all the poor from the Old Quarter;
women in aprons with cooking-pots on their shoulders, paralysed
old men in bath-chairs, cripples on crutches, all surrounded by
flocks of little boys.

When they got to the rocks at the headland, the mine was
thrown into the sea at a point where it was quickly carried off
shorewards on the tide. Out of the old violin case Grimpante
brought one of those guns that fire in bursts, and set it up behind
some rocks. When the mine was within range he began firing:
the shots sent up a shower of little jets on the water. The poor,

prostrate on their stomachs along the coast road, stopped up their ears.

Suddenly a great column of water rose from the sea where the mine had last been seen. The explosion was tremendous. It shattered all the windows of the surrounding villas. The wave that followed reached as far as the road. Hardly had the sea abated than the surface of the water was covered with the floating white stomachs of fish. Old Baci and Grimpante were trying to throw out a big net when they were overtaken by the crowd rushing down towards the sea.

The poor ran into the water fully dressed, some with shoes in their hands and trousers tucked up, others wearing shoes and all, women with their skirts floating round them in circles, all snatching at dead fish.

They took them with their hands, or hats, or shoes, stuffed them into their pockets and handbags. The boys were the quickest. But nobody jostled anyone else, as they'd all agreed to share out the fish in equal parts. They even helped the old people, who every now and then slipped under water and emerged with beards hung with seaweed and shrimps. The most fortunate were the nuns, who worked in pairs, with their veils spread out on the surface, sweeping the sea clean all round. Every now and again a pretty girl shrieked " Hi! Hi! " as a dead fish slipped under her skirts and a young man dived to retrieve it.

Fires made of dry seaweed were now lit on the beach, and cooking-pots brought out. Little bottles of oil were pulled from pockets, and very soon the air was filled with the smell of frying fish. Grimpante had slipped quietly away in case the police found him with that fire-arm in his possession. But old Baci was there in the middle of the crowd, with fish, crabs and prawns oozing out of every ragged tear in his clothes, contentedly chewing away at a raw mullet.

The Argentine Ant

WHEN WE came to settle here we did not know about the ants. We'd be all right here, it seemed that day; the sky and green looked bright, too bright, perhaps, for the worries we had, my wife and I—how could we have guessed about the ants? Thinking it over, though, Uncle Augusto may have hinted at this once: " You should see the ants over there . . . they're not like the ones here, those ants . . ." but that was just said while talking of something else, a remark of no importance, thrown in perhaps because as we talked we happened to notice some ants. Ants did I say? No, just one single lost ant, one of those fat ants we have at home (they seem fat to me, now, the ants from my part of the country). Anyway, Uncle Augusto's hint did not seem to detract from the description he gave us of a region where, for some reason which he was unable to explain, life was easier and jobs not too difficult to find, judging by all those who had set themselves up there— though not, apparently, Uncle Augusto himself.

On our first evening here, noticing the twilight still in the air after supper, realising how pleasant it was to stroll along those lanes towards the country and sit on the low walls of a bridge, we began to understand why Uncle Augusto liked it. We understood it even more when we found a little inn which he used to frequent, with a garden behind, and squat, elderly characters like himself, though rather more blustering and noisy, who said they

155

had been his friends; they too were men without a trade, I think, workers by the hour, though one said he was a clockmaker, but that may have been bragging; and we found they remembered Uncle Augusto by a nickname, which they all repeated among general guffaws; we noticed, too, rather stifled laughter from a woman in a knitted white jumper who was fat and no longer young, standing behind the bar.

And my wife and I understood what all this must have meant to Uncle Augusto; to have a nickname and spend light evenings joking on the bridges and watch for that knitted jumper to come from the kitchen and go out into the orchard, then spend an hour or two next day unloading sacks for the spaghetti factory; yes, we realised why he always regretted this place when he was back home.

I would have been able to appreciate all this too, if I'd been a youth and had no worries, or been well settled with the family. But as we were, with the baby only just recovered from his illness, and work still to find, we could do no more than notice the things that had made Uncle Augusto call himself happy; and just noticing them was perhaps rather sad, for it made us feel the difference between our own wretched state and the contented world around. Little things, often of no importance, worried us in case they suddenly made matters worse (before we knew anything about the ants); the endless instructions given us by the owner, Signora Mauro, while showing us over the rooms, increased this feeling we had of entering difficult waters. I remember a long talk she gave us about the gas-meter, and how carefully we listened to what she said.

" Yes, Signora Mauro . . . We'll be very careful, Signora Mauro . . . Let's hope not, Signora Mauro. . . ."

So that we did not take any notice when (though we remember it clearly now) she gave a quick glance all over the wall as if reading something there, then passed the tip of her finger over it, and brushed it afterwards as if she had touched something wet, sandy or dusty. She did not mention the word "ants," though, I'm certain of that; perhaps she considered it natural for ants to be there in the walls and roof; but my wife and I think now that she was trying to hide them from us as long as possible and that all her chatter and instructions were just a smokescreen to make other things seem important, and so direct our attention away from the ants.

When the Signora Mauro had gone, I carried the mattresses inside. My wife wasn't able to move the cupboard by herself and called me to help. Then she wanted to begin cleaning out the little kitchen at once and got down on her knees to start, but I said: "What's the point, at this hour? We'll see about that to-morrow; let's just arrange as best we can for to-night." The baby was whimpering and very sleepy, and the first thing to do was get his basket ready and put him to bed. At home we use a long basket for babies, and had brought one with us here; we emptied out the linen with which we'd filled it, and found a good place on the window-ledge, where it wasn't damp or too far off the ground should it fall.

Our son soon went off to sleep, and my wife and I began looking over our new home (one room divided in two by a partition—four walls and a roof); which was already showing signs of our occupation. "Yes, yes, whitewash it, of course we must white-wash it," I replied to my wife, glancing at the ceiling and at the same time taking her outside by an elbow. She wanted to have another good look at the lavatory, which was in a little hut to the left, but I wanted to take a turn over the surrounding plot; for our house stood on a piece of land consisting of two large flower-, or rather rough seed-beds, with a path down the middle covered with an iron trellis, now bare and made perhaps for some dried-up rambling plant of gourds or vines. The Signora Mauro had said she would let me have this plot to cultivate as a kitchen garden, without asking any rent, as it had been abandoned for so long; she had not mentioned this to us to-day, however, and we had not said anything as there were already too many other irons in the fire.

My intention now, by this first evening's walk of ours round the plot, was to acquire a sense of familiarity with the place, even of ownership in a way; for the first time in our lives the idea of continuity seemed possible, of walking evening after evening among beds of seeds as our circumstances gradually improved. Of course I didn't speak of those things to my wife; but I was anxious to see whether she felt them too; and that stroll of ours did, in fact, seem to have the effect on her which I had hoped. We began talking quietly, between long pauses, and we linked arms—a gesture symbolic of happier times.

Strolling along like this we came to the end of the plot, and over the hedge saw our neighbour, Signor Reginaudo, busy spraying round the outside of his house with a pair of bellows. I had met Signor Reginaudo a few months earlier when I had come to discuss my tenancy with the Signora Mauro. I went up to greet him and introduce him to my wife. "Good evening, Signor Reginaudo," I said. "D'you remember me?"

"Of course I do," he said. "Good evening! So you are our new neighbour now?" He was a short man with spectacles, in pyjamas and a straw hat.

"Yes, neighbours, and among neighbours. . . ." My wife began producing a few vague pleasant phrases, to be polite: it was a long time since I'd heard her talk like that; I didn't particularly like it, but it was better than hearing her complain.

"Claudia," called our neighbour, "come here. Here are the new tenants of the Casa Laureri!" I had never heard our new home called that (Laureri, I learnt later, was a previous owner), and the name made it sound strange. The Signora Reginaudo, a big woman, now came out, drying her hands on her apron; they were an easy-going couple and very friendly.

"And what are you doing there with those bellows, Signor Reginaudo?" I asked him.

" Oh . . . the ants . . . these ants . . ." he said, and laughed as if not wanting to make it sound important.

" Ants?" repeated my wife in the polite detached tone she used with strangers to give the impression she was paying attention to what they were saying; a tone she never used with me, not even, as far as I can remember, when we first met.

We then took a ceremonious leave of our neighbours. But we did not seem to be enjoying really fully the fact of having neighbours, and such affable and friendly ones to whom we could chat so pleasantly.

On getting home we decided to go to bed at once. "D'you hear?" said my wife. I listened and could hear still the squeak of Signor Reginaudo's bellows. My wife went to the wash-basin for a glass of water. "Bring me one too," I called, and took off my shirt.

"Ooooh!" she screamed. "Come here!" She had seen ants on the tap and a stream of them coming up the wall.

We put on the light, a single bulb for the two rooms. The stream of ants on the wall was very thick; they were coming from the top of the door, and might originate anywhere. Our hands were now covered with them, and we held them out open in front of our eyes, trying to see exactly what they were like, these ants, moving our wrists all the time to prevent them crawling up our arms. They were tiny wisps of ants, in ceaseless movement as if urged along by the same little itch they gave us. It was only then that a name came to my mind: "Argentine ants," or rather, "the Argentine ant," that's what they called them; and now I came to think of it I must have heard someone saying that this was the part of "the Argentine ant." It was only now that I connected the name with a sensation, this irritating tickle spreading in every direction, which one couldn't get rid of by clenching one's fists or rubbing one's hands together as there always seemed to be some stray ant running up one's arm, or on one's clothes. When the ants were crushed, they became little black dots which fell like sand, leaving a strong acid smell on one's fingers.

"It's the Argentine ant, you know . . ." I said to my wife. "It comes from South America. . . ." Unconsciously my voice had taken on the inflection I used when wanting to teach her something; as soon as I'd realised this I was sorry, for I knew that she could not bear that tone in my voice and always reacted sharply, perhaps sensing that I was never very sure of myself when using it.

But instead she scarcely seemed to have heard me; she was frenziedly trying to destroy or disperse that stream of ants on the wall, but all she managed to do was get numbers of them on herself and scatter others around. Then she put her hand under the tap and tried to squirt water at them, but the ants went on walking over the wet surface; she couldn't even get them off by washing her hands.

"There, we've ants in the house, there!" she repeated. "They were here before, too, and we didn't see them!"—as if things would have been very different if we had seen them before.

I said to her: "Oh, come, just a few ants! Let's go to bed now and think about it to-morrow!" And it occurred to me also to add: "Oh, just a few Argentine ants!" because by calling them by the exact name I wanted to suggest that their presence was already expected, and in a certain sense normal.

But the expansive feeling by which my wife had let herself be carried away during that stroll round the garden had now completely vanished; she had become distrustful of everything again and pulled her usual face. Nor was going to bed in our new home what I had hoped; we hadn't the pleasure now of feeling we were starting a new life, only a sense of dragging on into a future full of new troubles.

"All for a couple of ants," was what I was thinking—what I thought I was thinking, rather, for everything seemed different now for me too.

Exhaustion finally overcame our agitation, and we dozed off. But in the middle of the night the baby cried; at first we lay there in bed, always hoping it might stop and go to sleep again; this, however, never happened and we began asking ourselves: "What can be the matter? What's up with him?" Since he was better he had stopped crying at night.

"He's covered with ants!" cried my wife, who had gone and taken him in her arms. I got out of bed too. We turned the whole basket upside down and undressed the baby completely. To get enough light for picking the ants off, half blind as we were from sleep, we had to stand under the bulb in the draught coming from the door. My wife was saying: "Now he'll catch cold." It was pitiable looking for ants on that skin which reddened as soon as it was rubbed. There was a stream of ants going along the window-sill. We searched all the sheets until we could not find another ant and then said: "Where shall we put him to sleep now?" In our bed we were so squeezed up against each other we would have crushed him. I inspected the chest of drawers, and as the ants had not got into that, pulled it away from the wall, opened a drawer, and prepared a bed for the baby there. When we put him in he had already gone off to sleep. We had only to throw ourselves on the bed and would have soon dozed off again, but my wife wanted to look at our provisions.

"Come here, come here! God! Full of 'em! Everything's black! Help!" What was to be done? I took her by the shoulders. "Come along, we'll think about that to-morrow, we can't even see now, to-morrow we'll arrange everything, we'll put it all in a safe place, now come back to bed!"

"But the food. It'll be ruined!"

"It can go to the devil! What can we do now? To-morrow we'll destroy the ants' nest. Don't worry."

But we could no longer find peace in bed, with the thought of those insects everywhere, in the food, in all our things; perhaps by now they had crawled up the legs of the chest of drawers and reached the baby. . . . We got off to sleep as the cocks were crowing, but before long we had again started moving about and scratching ourselves and feeling we had ants in the bed; perhaps they had climbed up there, or stayed on us after all our handling of them. And so even the early morning hours were no refreshment, and we were very soon up, nagged by the thought of the things we had to do, and of the nuisance, too, of having to start an immediate battle against the persistent imperceptible enemy which had taken over our home.

The first thing my wife did was see to the baby; examine him for any bites (luckily there did not seem to be any), dress and feed him—all this while moving around in the ant-infested house. I knew the effort of self-control she was making not to let out a scream every time she saw, for example, ants going round the rims of the cups left in the sink, and the baby's bib, and the fruit. She did scream, though, when she uncovered the milk: " It's black! " There was a veil on top of drowned or swimming ants. " It's all on the surface," I said. " One can skim them off with a spoon." But even so we did not enjoy the milk; it seemed to taste of ants.

I followed the stream of ants on the walls to see where they came from. My wife was combing and dressing herself, with occasional little cries of hastily suppressed anger. " We can't arrange the furniture till we've got rid of the ants," she said.

" Keep calm. I'll see that everything is all right. I'm just going to Signor Reginaudo, who has that powder, and ask him for a little of it. We'll put the powder at the mouth of the ants' nest. I've already seen where it is, and we'll soon be free of them. But let's wait till a little later as we may be disturbing the Reginaudos at this hour."

My wife calmed down a little, but I didn't. I had said I'd seen the entrance to the ants' nest to console her, but the more I looked, the more new ways I discovered by which the ants came and went. Our new home, although it looked as smooth and solid on the surface, was in fact porous and honeycombed with cracks and holes.

I consoled myself by standing on the threshold and gazing at the plants with the sun pouring down on them; even the brushwood covering the ground cheered me as it made me long to get to work on it: to clean everything up thoroughly, then hoe and sow and transplant. " Come," I said to my son. " You're going mouldy here." I took him in my arms and went out into the " garden." Just for the pleasure of starting the habit of calling it that, I said to my wife: " I'm taking the baby into the garden for a moment," then corrected myself: " Into our garden," as that seemed even more possessive and familiar.

The baby was happy in the sunshine and I told him: " This is a carob tree, this is a custard apple," and lifted him up on to the branches. " Now Papa will teach you to climb." He burst out crying. " What's the matter? Are you frightened?" But I saw the ants; the sticky tree was covered with them. I pulled the baby down at once. " Oh, lots of dear little ants . . ." I said to him, but meanwhile, deep in thought, I was following the line of ants down the trunk, and saw that the silent and almost invisible swarm continued along the ground in every direction between the weeds. How, I was beginning to wonder, shall we ever be able to get the ants out of the house when over this piece of ground, which had seemed so small yesterday but now appeared enormous in relation to the ants, the insects formed an uninterrupted veil, issuing from what must be thousands of underground nests and feeding on the thick sticky soil and the low vegetation? Wherever I looked I'd see nothing at first glance and would be giving a sigh of relief; when I'd look closer and discover an ant approaching and find it formed part of a long procession, and was meeting others, often carrying crumbs and tiny bits of material much larger than themselves. In certain places, where they had perhaps collected some plant juice or animal remains, there was a guarding crust of ants stuck together like the black scab of a wound.

I returned to my wife with the baby at my neck, almost at a run, feeling the ants climbing up me from my feet. And she said: "Look, you've made the baby cry. What's the matter?"

"Nothing, nothing," I said hurriedly. "He saw a couple of ants on a tree and is still affected by last night, and thinks he's itching."

"Oh, to have this to put up with too!" my wife cried. She was following a line of ants on the wall and trying to kill them by pressing the ends of her fingers on each one. I could still see the millions of ants surrounding us on that plot of ground, which now seemed immeasurable to me, and found myself shouting at her angrily: "What're you doing? Are you mad? You won't get anything done that way."

She burst out in a flash of rage too. "But Uncle Augusto! Uncle Augusto never said a word to us! What a couple of fools we were? To pay any attention to that old liar!" In fact, what could Uncle Augusto have told us? The word "ants" for us then could never have even suggested the horror of our present condition. If he had mentioned ants, as perhaps he had—I won't exclude the possibility—we would have imagined ourselves up against a concrete enemy, that could be numbered, weighed, crushed. Actually, now I think about the ants in our own parts, I remember them as reasonable little creatures, which could be touched and moved like cats or rabbits. Here we were face to face with an enemy like fog or sand, against which force was useless.

Our neighbour, Signor Reginaudo, was in his kitchen pouring liquid through a funnel. I called him from outside, and reached the kitchen window panting hard.

"Ah, our neighbour!" exclaimed Reginaudo. "Come in, come in. Forgive this mess! Claudia, a chair for our neighbour."

I said to him quickly: "I've come . . . please forgive the intrusion, but you know, I saw that you had some of that powder . . . all last night, the ants . . ."

" Oh, oh . . . the ants!" The Signora Reginaudo burst out laughing as she came in, and her husband echoed her with a slight delay, it seemed to me, though his guffaws were noisier when they came. " Ha, ha, ha! . . . You have ants, too! Hah, hah, hah!"

Without wanting to, I found myself giving a modest smile, as if realising how ridiculous my situation was, but now I could do nothing about it; this was in point of fact true, as I'd had to come and ask for help.

" Ants! You don't say so, my dear neighbour!" exclaimed Signor Reginaudo, raising his hands.

" You don't say so, dear neighbour, you don't say so!" exclaimed his wife, pressing her hands to her breast but still laughing with her husband.

" But you have a remedy, haven't you?" I asked, and the quiver in my voice could, perhaps, have been taken for a longing to laugh, and not for the despair I could feel coming over me.

" A remedy, hah, hah, hah!" the Reginaudos laughed louder than ever. " Have we a remedy? We've twenty remedies! A hundred . . . Each, ha, ha, ha . . . each better than the other!"

They led me into another room lined with dozens of cartons and tins with brilliant coloured labels.

" D'you want some Profosfan? Or Mirminec? Or perhaps Titobrofit? Or Arsopan in powder or liquid form?" And still roaring with laughter he passed his hand over sprinklers with pistons, brushes, sprays, raising clouds of yellow dust, tiny beads of moisture, and a smell which was a mixture of a chemist's shop and an agricultural depot.

" Have you really anything that does the job?" I asked.

They stopped laughing. " No, nothing," he replied.

Signor Reginaudo patted me on the shoulder, the Signora opened the blinds to let the sun in. Then they took me round the house.

He was wearing pyjama trousers with red cords knotted over his fat little stomach, and a straw hat on his bald head. She wore a

165

faded dressing-gown, which opened every now and then to reveal the shoulder straps of her under-vest; the hair round her big red face was fair, dry, curly and dishevelled. They both talked loudly and expansively; every corner of their house had a story which they recounted, repeating and interrupting each other with gestures and exclamations as if each episode had been a jolly farce. In one place they had put down Arfanax at two to a thousand and the ants had vanished for two days, but returned on the third day; then he had concentrated the liquid ten to a thousand, but the ants had simply avoided that part and circled round by the door-frame; they had isolated another corner with Crisotan powder, but the wind blew it away and they used three kilos a day; on the stairs they had tried Petrocid, which seemed at first to kill them at one blow, but instead it had only sent them to sleep; in another corner they put down Formikill and the ants went on passing over it, then one morning they found a mouse poisoned there; in one spot they had put down liquid Zimofosf, which had acted as a definite blockade, but his wife had put Italmac powder on top which had acted as an antidote and completely nullified the effect. Our neighbours used their house and garden as a battlefield, and their passion was to trace lines beyond which the ants could not pass, to discover the new detours they made, and to try out new mixtures and powders, each of which was linked to the memory of some strange episode or comic occurrence, so that one of them only had to pronounce a name—" Arsepit! Mirxidol!"—for them both to burst out laughing with winks and comments. As for the actual killing of the ants, that, if they had ever attempted it, they seemed to have given up, seeing that their efforts were useless; all they tried to do was bar them from certain passages and deviate, frighten or to keep them at bay. They always had a new labyrinth traced out with different substances which they prepared from day to day, and for this game ants were a necessary element.

" There's nothing else to be done with the creatures, nothing," they said, " unless one deals with them like the captain . . ."

" Ah, yes, we certainly spend a lot of money on these insecticides," they said. " The captain's system is much more economical, you know."

" Of course, we can't say we've defeated the Argentine ant yet," they added, " but d'you really think that captain is on the right road? I doubt it."

" Excuse me," I asked. " But who is the captain?"

" Captain Brauni; don't you know him? Oh, of course, you only arrived yesterday! He's our neighbour there on the right, in that little white villa . . . an inventor. . . ." They laughed. " He's invented a system to exterminate the Argentine ant . . . lots of systems, in fact. And he's still perfecting them. Go and see him."

The Reginaudos stood there, plump and sly among their few square yards of garden which was daubed all over with streaks and splashes of dark liquids, sprinkled with greenish powder, encumbered with watering cans, fumigators, cement jars filled with some indigo-coloured preparation; in the disordered flower-beds were a few little rose-bushes covered with insecticide from the tips of the leaves to the roots. The Reginaudos raised contented and amused eyes to the limpid sky. Talking to them I found myself slightly heartened; although the ants were not just something to laugh at as they seemed to think, neither were they so terribly serious, anything to lose heart about. " Oh, the ants!" I now thought. " Just ants after all! What harm can a few ants do?" Now I'd go back to my wife and tease her a bit: " What on earth d'you think you've seen, with those ants . . . ?"

I was mentally preparing a talk in this tone while returning across our piece of ground with my arms full of cartons and tins lent by our neighbours for us to choose the ones that wouldn't harm the baby, who put everything in its mouth. But when I saw my wife outside the house holding the baby, her eyes glassy and her cheeks hollow, and realised the battle she must have fought, I lost all desire to smile and joke.

" At last you've come back," she said, and her quiet tone hit

me more painfully than the angry accent I had expected. " I didn't
know what to do here any more . . . if you saw . . . I really
didn't know . . ."

" Look, now we can try this," I said to her, " and this and this
and this . . ." and I put down my cans on the step in front of the
house, and at once began hurriedly explaining how they were to
be used, almost afraid of seeing too much hope rising in her eyes
in case I deceived or disallusioned her. Now I had another idea;
I wanted to go at once and see that Captain Brauni.

" Carry on as I've explained; I'll be back in a minute."

" You're going away again? Where are you off to?"

" To another neighbour's. He has a system. You'll see soon."
And I ran off towards a metal railing covered with ramblers
bounding our land to the right. The sun was behind a cloud.
I looked through the railings and saw a little white villa surrounded by a tiny neat garden, with gravel paths encircling flower-
beds, bordered by wrought-iron painted green as in public gardens,
and in the middle of every flower-bed a little black orange or
lemon tree. Everything was quiet, shady and still. I was standing
there, uncertain whether to go away, when, bending over a well-
clipped hedge, I saw a head covered with a shapeless white linen
beach hat, pulled forward to a wavy brim above a pair of steel-
framed glasses on a spongy nose, and then a sharp flashing smile
of false teeth, also made of steel. He was a thin, shrivelled man in
a pullover, with trousers clamped at the ankles by bicycle clips,
and sandals on his feet. He went up to examine the trunk of one of
the orange trees, looking silent and circumspect, still with his
tight-lipped smile. I looked out from behind the rambler and
called: " Good day, Captain." The man raised his head with a
start, no longer smiling, and gave me a cold stare.

" Excuse me, are you Captain Brauni?" I asked him. The man
nodded. " I'm the new neighbour, you know, who's rented the
Casa Laureri. . . . May I trouble you for a moment as I've heard
that your system . . ."

The captain raised a finger and beckoned me to come nearer; I jumped through a gap in the iron trellis. The captain was still holding up his finger, while pointing with the other hand to the spot he was observing. I saw that hanging from the tree, perpendicular to the trunk, was a short iron wire. At the end of the wire hung a piece—it seemed to me—of fish remains, and in the middle was a bulge at an acute angle pointing downwards. A stream of ants was going to and fro on the trunk and the wire. Underneath the end of the wire was hanging a sort of meat tin.

" The ants," explained the captain, " attracted by the smell of fish, run across the piece of wire; as you see, they can go to and fro on it without bumping into each other. But it's that V turn which is dangerous; when an ant going up meets one coming down on the turn of the V, they both stop, and the smell of the petrol in this can stuns them; they try to go on their way, but bump into each other, fall and are drowned in the petrol. Tic, tic." (This " tic tic " accompanied the fall of two ants.) " Tic, tic, tic . . ." continued the captain with his steely, stiff smile; and every " tic " accompanied the fall of an ant into the can where, on the surface of an inch of petrol, lay a black crust of shapeless insect bodies.

" An average of forty ants are killed per minute," said Captain Brauni, " 2,400 per hour. Naturally, the petrol must be kept clean, otherwise the dead ants cover it and the ones that fall in afterwards can save themselves."

I could not take my eyes off that thin but regular trickle of ants dropping off; many of them got over the dangerous point and returned dragging bits of fish back with them by the teeth, but there was always one which stopped at that point, waved its antennae and then plunged into the depths. Captain Brauni, with a fixed stare behind his lenses, did not miss the slightest movement of the insects; at every fall he gave a tiny uncontrollable start and the tightly stretched corners of his almost lipless mouth twitched. Often he could not resist putting out his hands, either to correct the angle of the wire or to swill the petrol round the crust of dead ants on the sides, or even to give his instruments a little shake to accelerate the victims' fall. But this last gesture must have almost seemed to him like breaking the rules, for he quickly drew back his hand and looked at me as if to justify his action.

"This is an improved model," he said, leading me to another tree from which hung a wire with a horse-hair tied to the vertical of the V: the ants thought they could save themselves on the horse-hair, but the smell of the petrol and the unexpectedly tenuous support confused them to the point of making the fatal drop. This expedient of the bristle or horse-hair was applied to many other traps that the captain showed me; a third piece of wire would suddenly end in a piece of thin horse-hair, and the ants would be confused by the change and lose their balance; he had even constructed a trap by which the corner was reached over a bridge made of a half broken bristle, which opened under the weight of the ant and let it fall in the petrol.

Applied with mathematical precision to every tree, every piece of tubing, every balustrade and column in this silent and neat garden, were wire contraptions with cans of petrol underneath, and the well potted rose trees and lattice work of ramblers seemed only a careful camouflage for this parade of executions.

"Aglaura!" cried the captain, going up to the kitchen door, and to me: "Now I'll show you our catch for the last few days."

Out of the door came a tall, thin, pale woman with frightened, malevolent eyes, and a handkerchief knotted down over her forehead.

"Show our neighbour the sack," said Brauni, and I realised she was not a servant but the captain's wife, and greeted her with a nod and a murmur, but she did not reply. She went into the house and came out again dragging a heavy sack along the ground, her muscular arms showing a greater strength than I had attributed to her at first glance. Through the half-closed door I could see a pile of sacks like this one stacked about; the woman had disappeared, still without saying a word.

The captain opened the mouth of the sack; it looked as if it contained garden mould or chemical manure, but he put his arm in and brought out a handful of what seemed to be coffee grounds and let this trickle into his other hand; they were dead ants, a soft red-black sand of dead ants all rolled up in tight little balls, reduced to spots in which one could no longer distinguish the head from the legs. They gave out a pungent acid smell. In the house there were hundredweights, pyramids of sacks like this one, all full.

" It's incredible," I said. " You've exterminated all of these, so . . ."

" No," said the captain calmly. " It's no use killing the worker ants. There are ants' nests everywhere with queen ants which breed millions of others."

" What then ? "

I squatted down beside the sack; he was seated on a step below me and to speak to me had to raise his head; the shapeless brim of his white hat covered the whole of his forehead and part of his round spectacles.

" The queens must be starved. If you reduce to a minimum the number of workers taking food to the ants' nests, the queens will be left without enough to eat. And I tell you that one day we'll see the queens come out of their ants' nests in high summer and crawl round searching for food with her own claws. . . . That'll be the end of them all, and then . . ."

He shut the mouth of the sack with an excited gesture and got up. I got up too. " But some people think they can solve it by letting the ants escape." He threw a glance towards the Reginaudos' little house, and showed his steel-teeth in a contemptuous laugh. " And there are even those who prefer fattening them up. . . . That's one way of dealing with them, isn't it ? "

I did not understand his second allusion.

"Who?" I asked. "Why should anyone want to fatten them up?"

"Hasn't the ant-man been to you?"

What man did he mean? "I don't know," I said. "I don't think so . . ."

"Don't worry, he'll come to you too. He usually comes on Thursdays, so if he wasn't here this morning he will be in the afternoon. To give the ants a tonic, hah, hah!"

I smiled to please him, but did not follow. Then as I had come to him with a purpose I said: "I'm sure yours is the best possible system. D'you think I could try it at my place too?"

"Just tell me which model you prefer," said Brauni, and led me back into the garden. There were numbers of his inventions which I had not yet seen. Swinging wire, which when loaded with ants made contact with a battery that electrocuted the lot; anvils and hammers covered with honey which clashed together at the release of a spring and squashed all the ants left in between; wheels with teeth which the ants themselves put in motion, tearing their brethren to pieces until they in their turn were churned up by the pressure of those coming after. I couldn't get used to the idea of so much art and perseverance being needed to carry out such a simple operation as catching ants; but I realised that the important thing was to carry on continually and methodically. Then I felt discouraged as no one, it seemed to me, could ever equal this neighbour of ours in terrible determination.

"Perhaps one of the simpler models would be best for us," I said, and Brauni snorted, I didn't know whether from approval, or sympathy with the modesty of my ambition.

"I must think a bit about it," he said. "I'll do some sketches."

There was nothing else left for me to do but thank him and take my leave. I went back over the hedge; my house, infested as it was, I felt for the first time to be really my home, a place where one returned saying: "Here I am at last."

But at home the baby had eaten the insecticide and my wife was in despair.

"Don't worry, it's not poisonous!" I quickly said.

No, it wasn't poisonous, but it wasn't good to eat either; our son was screaming with pain. He had to be made to vomit; he vomited in the kitchen, which at once filled with ants again, and my wife had just cleaned it up. We washed the floor, calmed the baby, and put him to sleep in the basket, isolated him all round with insect powder, and covered him with a mosquito net tied tight, so that if he awoke he couldn't get up and eat any more of the stuff.

My wife had done the shopping but had not been able to save the basket from the ants, so everything had to be washed first, even the sardines-in-oil and the cheese, and each ant sticking to them picked off one by one. I helped her, chopped the wood, tidied the kitchen and fixed the stove, while she cleaned the vegetables. But it was impossible to stand still in one place; every minute either she or I jumped and said: " Ooooh! it's biting " —and we had to scratch ourselves and rub off the ants or put our arms and legs under the tap. We did not know where to lay the table; inside it would attract more ants, outside we'd be covered with ants in no time. We ate standing up, moving about, and everything tasted of ants, partly from the ones still left in the food and partly because our hands were impregnated with their smell.

After eating I made a tour of the piece of land, smoking a cigarette. From the Reginaudos' came a tinkling of knives and forks; I leant over and saw them sitting at table under an umbrella, looking shiny and calm, with checked napkins tied round their throats, eating a cream pudding and drinking glasses of clear wine. I wished them a good appetite and they invited me to join them. But round the table I saw sacks and cans of insecticide, and everything covered with nets sprinkled with yellowish or whitish powder, and that smell of chemicals rose to my nostrils. I thanked them and said I no longer had any appetite, which was true. The Reginaudos' radio was playing softly and they were chattering in high voices, pretending to toast themselves.

From the steps which I'd gone up to greet them I could also see a piece of the Brauni's garden; the captain must already have finished eating; he was coming out of his house with his cup and saucer of coffee, sipping and glancing around, obviously to see if all his instruments of torture were in action and if the ants' death-agonies were continuing with their usual regularity. Suspended between two trees I saw a white hammock, and realised that the bony, disagreeable-looking Signora Aglaura must be lying in it, though I could see only a wrist and a hand waving a cardboard fan. The hammock ropes were suspended in a system of strange rings, which must certainly have been some sort of defence against the ants; or perhaps the hammock itself was a trap for the ants, with the captain's wife put there as bait.

I did not want to discuss my visit to the Braunis with the Reginaudos, as I knew they would only have made the ironic comments that seemed usual in the relations between our neighbours. I looked up at the Signora Mauro's garden above us on the crest of the hills, and at her villa surmounted by a revolving weathercock. "I wonder if the Signora Mauro has ants up there too," I said.

The Reginaudos' gaiety seemed rather more subdued during their meal; they only gave a little quiet laugh or two and said no more than: "Hah, hah, she must have them too. Hah, hah, yes, she must have them, lots of them. . . ."

My wife called me back to the house, as she wanted to put a mattress on the table and try and get a little sleep. With the mattresses on the floor it was impossible to prevent the ants from crawling up, but with the table we just had to isolate the four feet to keep them off, for a bit at least. She lay down to rest and I went out, intending to look for some people who might put me on to a job, but really because I longed to move about and change the course of my thoughts.

But as I went along the road, things around seemed different from yesterday; in every kitchen garden, in every house I sensed streams of ants climbing the walls, covering the fruit trees, wriggling their antennae towards everything sweet or greasy; and my newly trained eyes now noticed at once mattresses put outside houses to beat because the ants had got into them, a spray of insecticide in an old woman's hand, a saucerful of poison, and then, straining my eyes, the rows of ants marching imperturbably round the cornices of the doors.

And yet this part had still been Uncle Augusto's ideal. Unloading sacks, an hour for one employer and an hour for another, eating on the benches at the inn, going round in the evening in search of gaiety and a mouth organ, sleeping wherever he happened to be, wherever it was fresh and soft, what bother could the ants have been to him?

As I walked along I tried to imagine myself as Uncle Augusto and to move along the road as he would have done on an afternoon like this. Of course, being like Uncle Augusto meant first being like him physically: squat and sturdy, that is, with rather monkey-like arms that opened and stayed in mid-air in disproportionate gestures, and short legs which stumbled when he turned to look at a girl, and a voice which when he got excited repeated the local slang all out of tune with his own accent. In him body and soul were all one; how nice it would have been, gloomy and worried as I was, to have been able to move and joke like Uncle Augusto. I could always pretend to be him mentally though, and say to myself: "What a sleep I'll have in that hayloft. What a bellyful of black pudding and wine I'll have at the inn!" I imagined myself pretending to stroke the cats I saw, then shouting "Booo!" to frighten them unexpectedly; and calling out to the servant-girls: "Hey, would you like me to come and give you a hand, Signorina?" But the game wasn't much fun; the more I tried to imagine how simple life was for Uncle Augusto here, the more I realised he was a different type, a man who never had my worries: a home to set up, a permanent job to find, an ailing baby, a long-faced wife, and a bed and kitchen full of ants.

I entered the inn where we had already been, and asked the girl in the white jumper if the men I'd talked to the day before had come yet. It was shady and cool in there; perhaps it wasn't a place for ants. I sat down to wait for those men, as she suggested, and asked, looking as careless as I could: " So you haven't any ants here, then? "

She was passing a duster over the counter. " Oh, people come and go here, no one's ever paid any attention."

" But what about you who live here all the time? "

The girl shrugged her shoulders. " I'm grown up, why should I be frightened of ants? "

Her air of dismissing the ants, as if they were something to be ashamed of, irritated me more and more, and I insisted: " But don't you put any poison down? "

" The best poison against ants," said a man sitting at another table, who, I noted now, was one of those friends of Uncle Augusto's to whom I'd spoken the evening before, " is this here," and he raised his glass and drank it in one gulp.

Others came in and wanted to stand me a drink as they hadn't been able to put me on to any jobs. We talked about Uncle Augusto and one of them asked: " And what's that old *lingera* up to? " " *Lingera* " is a local word meaning vagabond and gallows-bird, and they all seemed to approve of this definition of him and to hold my uncle in great esteem as a *lingera*. I was a little confused at this reputation being attributed to a man whom I knew to be in fact considerate and modest, in spite of his dis-ordered way of life. But perhaps this was part of the boasting, exaggerated attitude common to all these people, and it occurred to me in a confused sort of way that this was somehow linked with the ants, that pretending they lived in a world of great movement and adventure was a way of insulating themselves from petty annoyances.

What prevented me from entering their state of mind—I was thinking on my way home—was my wife, who had always been opposed to any fantasy. And I thought what an influence she had had on my life, and how nowadays I could never get drunk on words and ideas any more.

She met me on the doorstep looking rather alarmed, and said: " Listen, there's a surveyor here." I, who still had in my ears the sound of superiority of those blusterers at the inn, said almost without listening: " What now, a surveyor . . . Well, I'll just . . ."

She went on: " A surveyor's come to take measurements." I did not understand and went in. " Ah, now I see. It's the captain! "

It was Captain Brauni who was taking measurements with a yellow tape measure, to set up one of his traps in our house. I introduced him to my wife and thanked him for his kindness.

" I wanted to have a look at the possibilities here," he said. " Everything must be done in a strictly mathematical way." He even measured the basket where the baby was sleeping, and woke it up. The child was frightened at seeing the yellow yardstick levelled over its head and began to cry. My wife tried to put it to sleep again. The baby's crying made the captain nervous, though I tried to distract him. Luckily he heard his wife calling him and went out. The Signora Aglaura was leaning over the hedge and shouting: " Come here! Come here! There's a visitor! Yes, the ant-man! "

Brauni gave me a glance and a meaning smile from his thin lips, and excused himself for having to return to his house so soon. " Now, he'll come to you too," he said, pointing towards the place where this mysterious ant-man was to be found. " You'll soon see," and he went away.

I did not want to find myself face to face with this ant-man without knowing exactly who he was and what he had come to do. I went to the steps which led to Reginaudo's land; our neighbour was just at that moment returning home; he was wearing a white coat and a straw hat, and was loaded with sacks and cartons. I said to him: " Tell me, the ant-man, has he been to you yet? "

" I don't know," said Reginaudo, " I've just got back, but I think he must have as I see molasses everywhere. Claudia! "

His wife leant out and said: " Yes, yes, he'll come to the Casa Laureri too, but don't expect him to do very much, you know! "

As if I was expecting anything at all! I asked: " But who sends this man? "

" Who sends him? " repeated Reginaudo. " He's the man from the Argentine Ant Control Corporation, their representative who comes and puts molasses all over the gardens and houses. Those little plates over there, do you see them? "

My wife said: " Poisoned molasses . . ." and gave a little laugh as if she expected trouble.

" Does it kill them? " These questions of mine were just a deprecating joke. I knew it all already. Every now and then everything would seem on the point of clearing up, then complications would begin all over again.

Signor Reginaudo shook his head as if I'd said something improper. " Oh no . . . just minute doses of poison, you understand . . . ants love sugary molasses. The worker ants take it back to the nest and feed the queens with these little doses of poison, so that sooner or later they're supposed to die from poisoning."

I did not want to ask if, sooner or later, they really did die. I realised that Signor Reginaudo was informing me of this proceeding in the tone of one who personally holds a different view, but feels that he should give an objective and respectful account of official opinion. His wife, however, with the usual intolerance of women, was quite open about showing her aversion to the molasses system and interrupted her husband's remarks with little malicious laughs and ironic comments; this attitude of hers must have seemed to him out of place or too open, for he tried by his voice and manner to attenuate her defeatism, though not actually contradicting her completely—perhaps because in private he said the same things, or worse—by making little balancing remarks such as: " Come now, you exaggerate, Claudia. . . . It's certainly not very effective, but it may help . . . Then, they do it for nothing. One must wait a year or two before judging. . . ."

" A year or two? They've been putting that stuff down for twenty years, and every year the ants multiply."

Signor Reginaudo, rather than contradict her, preferred to turn the conversation on to other services performed by the Corporation; and he told me about the boxes of manure which the ant-man put in the gardens for the queens to go and lay their eggs in, and how they then came and took them away to burn.

I realised that Signor Reginaudo's tone was the best to use in explaining matters to my wife, who is suspicious and pessimistic by nature, and when I got back home I reported what our neighbour had said, taking care not to praise the system as in any way miraculous or speedy, but also avoiding the Signora Claudia's ironical comments. My wife is one of those women who, when she goes by train, for example, thinks that the time-table, the position of the railway carriages, the requests of the ticket-collectors, are all stupid and ill-arranged, without any possible justification, but to be accepted with submissive rancour; so though she considered this business of molasses to be absurd and ridiculous, she made ready for the visit of the ant-man (who, I gathered, was called Signor Baudino), intending to make no protest or useless request for help.

The man entered our plot of land without asking permission and we found ourselves face to face while we were still talking about him, which caused rather an unpleasant embarrassment; he was a little man of about fifty, in a worn, faded black suit, with rather a drunkard's face, and hair that was still dark, worn in a childish fringe. Half-closed lids, a rather greasy little smile, reddish

179

skin round his eyes and at the sides of his nose, prepared us for the intonations of a clucking rather priest-like voice with a strong lilt of dialect. A nervous trick made the wrinkles pulsate at the corner of his mouth and nose.

If I describe Signor Baudino in such detail, it's to try and define the strange impression that he made on us; but was it strange, really? For it seemed to us that we'd have picked him out among thousands as the ant-man. He had large, hairy hands; in one he held a sort of coffee-pot and in the other a pile of little earthenware plates. He told us about the molasses he had to put down, and his voice betrayed a lazy indifference to the job; even the soft and dragging way he had of pronouncing the word " molasses " showed both disdain for the straits we were in and the complete distrust with which he carried out his task. I noticed that my wife was displaying exemplary calm as she showed him the main places where the ants passed. For myself, seeing him move so hesitantly, repeating again and again those few gestures of filling the dishes one after the other, nearly made me lose my patience. Watching him like that, I realised why he had made such a strange impression on me at first sight; he looked like an ant. It's difficult to tell exactly why, but he certainly did; perhaps it was because of the opaque black of his clothes and hair, perhaps because of the proportions of that squat body of his, or the trembling at the corners of his mouth corresponding to the continuous quiver of antennae and claws. There was, however, one characteristic of the ants which he had not got, and that was their continuous busy movement. Signor Baudino moved slowly and awkwardly, as he now began daubing the house in an aimless way with a brush dipped in molasses.

As I followed the man's movements with increasing irritation I noticed my wife was no longer with me; I looked round and saw her in a corner of the garden where the hedge of the Reginaudos' little house joined that of the Braunis'. Leaning over their respective hedges were the Signora Claudia and the Signora

Aglaura, deep in talk, with my wife standing in the middle listening. Signor Baudino was now working on the yard at the back of the house, where he could dirty as much as he liked without having to be watched, so I went up to the women and heard the Signora Brauni holding forth to the accompaniment of sharp angular gestures.

" He's come to give the ants a tonic, that man has; a tonic, not poison at all! "

The Signora Reginaudo now chimed in, rather mellifluously: "What will the employees of the Corporation do when there are no more ants? So what can you expect of them, my dear Signora?"

" They just fatten the ants, that's what they do! " concluded the Signora Aglaura angrily.

My wife stood listening quietly, as both the neighbours' remarks were addressed to her, but the way in which she was dilating her nostrils and curling her lips told me how furious she was at the deceit she was being forced to put up with. And I, too, I must say, found myself very near believing that this was more than women's gossip.

" And what about the boxes of manure for the eggs? " went on Signora Reginaudo. "They take them away, but do you think they'll burn them? Of course not! "

" Claudia, Claudia! " I heard her husband calling. Obviously these indiscreet remarks of his wife made him feel on tenter-hooks. The Signora Reginaudo left us with an " Excuse me," in which vibrated a note of disdain for her husband's conventionality, while I thought I heard a kind of sardonic laugh echoing back from over the other hedge, where I caught sight of Captain Brauni walking up the gravelled paths correcting the slant of his traps. One of the earthenware dishes just filled by Signor Baudino lay overturned and smashed at his feet by a kick which might have been accidental or intended.

I don't know what my wife had brewing up inside her against the ant-man as we were returning towards the house; probably at that moment I should have done nothing to stop her, and might even have supported her. But on glancing round the outside and inside of the house, we realised that Signor Baudino had disappeared; and I remembered hearing our gate creaking and shutting as we came along. He must have gone that moment without saying good-bye, leaving behind him those bowls of sticky, reddish molasses, which spread an unpleasant sweet smell, completely different from that of the ants, but somehow linked to it, I could not say how.

As our son was sleeping, we thought that now was the moment to go up and see Signora Mauro. We had to go and visit her, not only as a duty call but to ask her for the key of a certain store-room. The real reasons, though, why we were making this call so soon were to remonstrate with her for having rented us a place invaded with ants without warning us in any way, and chiefly to find out how our landlady defended herself against this scourge. Signora Mauro's villa had a big garden running up the slope under tall palms with yellowed fan-like leaves. A twisting path led to the house, which was all glass verandas and skylights, with a rusty weathercock turning creakily on its hinge on top of the roof, far less responsive to the wind than the palm leaves which waved and rustled at every gust. My wife and I climbed the path and gazed down from the balustrade at the little house where we lived and which was still unfamiliar to us, at our patch of uncultivated land and the Reginaudos' garden looking like a warehouse yard, at the Braunis' garden looking as set as a cemetery. And standing up there we could forget that all those places were black with ants; now we could see how they might have been without that menace which none of us could get away from even for an instant. At this distance it looked almost a paradise, but the more we gazed down the more we pitied our life there, as if living in that wretched narrow valley we could never get away from our wretched narrow problems.

The Signora Mauro was very old, thin and tall. She received us in half darkness, sitting on a high-backed chair by a little table which opened to hold sewing things and writing materials. She was dressed in black, except for a white masculine collar; her thin face was lightly powdered, and the hair drawn severely back. She immediately handed us the key she had promised us the day before, but did not ask if we were all right, and this—it seemed to us—was a sign that she was already expecting our complaints.

" But the ants that are down there, Signora . . ." said my wife in a tone which this time I wished had been less humble and resigned. Although she can be quite hard and often even aggressive, my wife is seized by shyness every now and then, and seeing her at these moments always makes me feel uncomfortable too.

I came to her support, and putting on a tone full of resentment, said: " You've rented us a house, Signora, which if I'd known about all those ants, I must tell you frankly . . ." and stopped there, thinking that I'd been clear enough.

The Signora did not even raise her eyes. " The house has been unoccupied for a long time," she said. " It's understandable that there are a few Argentine ants in it . . . they get wherever . . . wherever things aren't properly cleaned. You," she turned to me, " kept me waiting for four months before giving me a reply. If you'd taken the place immediately, there wouldn't be any ants by now."

We looked at the room, almost in darkness because of the half-closed blinds and curtains, at the high walls covered with antique tapestry, at the dark, inlaid furniture with the silver vases and teapots glimmering on top, and it seemed to us that this darkness and these heavy hangings served to hide the presence of streams of ants which must certainly be running through the old house from foundations to roof.

" And here . . ." said my wife, in an insinuating, almost ironical tone, " you haven't any ants? "

The Signora Mauro drew in her lips. " No," she said curtly; and then as if she felt she was not being believed, explained:

" Here we keep everything clean and shining as a mirror. As soon as any ants enter the garden, we realise it and deal with them at once."

" How?" my wife and I quickly asked in one voice, feeling only hope and curiosity now.

" Oh," said the Signora, shrugging her shoulders, " we chase them away, chase them away with brooms." At that moment her expression of studied impassiveness was shaken as if by a spasm of physical pain, and we saw that, as she sat, she suddenly moved her weight to another side of the chair and arched in her waist. Had it not contradicted her affirmations I'd have said that an Argentine ant was passing under her clothes and had just given her a bite; one or perhaps several ants were surely crawling up her body and making her itch, for in spite of her efforts not to move from the chair it was obvious that she was unable to remain calm and composed as before—she sat there tensely, while her face showed signs of sharper and sharper suffering.

" But that bit of land in front of us is black with 'em," I said hurriedly, " and however clean we keep the house, they come from the garden in their thousands. . . ."

" Of course," said the Signora, her thin hand closing over the arm of the chair, " of course it's rough uncultivated ground that makes the ants increase so; I intended to put the land in order four months ago. You made me wait, and now the damage is done; it's not only damaged you, but everyone else round, because the ants breed . . ."

" Don't they breed up here too?" asked my wife, almost smiling.

" No, not here!" said the Signora Mauro, going pale, then, still holding her right arm against the side of the chair, she began making a little rotating movement of the shoulder and rubbing her elbow against her ribs.

It occurred to me that the darkness, the ornaments, the size of the room and her proud spirit were this woman's defences against the ants, the reason why she was stronger than we were in face of them; but that everything we saw round us, beginning with her sitting there, was covered with ants even more pitiless than ours; some kind of African termite, perhaps, which destroyed everything and left only the husks, so that all that remained of this house were tapestries and curtains almost in powder, all on the point of crumbling into smithereens before her eyes.

" We really came to ask you if you could give us some advice how to get rid of the pests," said my wife, who was now completely self-possessed.

" Keep the house clean and dig away at the ground. There's no other remedy. Work, just work," and she got to her feet, the sudden decision to say good-bye to us coinciding with an instinctive start, as if she could keep still no longer. Then she composed herself and a shadow of relief passed over her pale face.

We went down through the garden, and my wife said: " Anyway let's hope the baby hasn't woken up." I, too, was thinking of the baby. Even before we reached the house we heard him crying. We ran, took him in our arms, and tried to quieten him, but he went on crying shrilly. An ant had got into his ear; we could not understand at first why he cried so desperately without any apparent reason. My wife had said at once: " It must be an ant! " but I could not understand why he went on crying so, as we could find no ants on him or any signs of bites or irritation, and we'd undressed and carefully inspected him. We found some in the basket, however; I'd done my very best to isolate it properly, but we had overlooked the ant-man's molasses—one of the clumsy streaks made by Signor Baudino seemed to have been put down on purpose to attract the insects up from the floor to the child's cot.

What with the baby's tears and my wife's cries, we had attracted all the neighbouring women to the house: the Signora Reginaudo, who was really very kind and sweet, the Signora Brauni, who, I must say, did everything she could to help us, and other women I'd never seen before. They all gave ceaseless advice; to pour warm oil in his ear, make him hold his mouth open, blow his nose, and I don't know what else. They screamed and shouted and ended by giving us more trouble than help, although they'd been a certain comfort at first; and the more they fussed round our baby the more bitter we all felt against the ant-man. My wife had blamed and cursed him to the four winds of heaven; and the neighbours all agreed with her that the man deserved all he'd get, and that he was doing all he could to help the ants increase so as not to lose his job, and that he was perfectly capable of having done this on purpose, because now he was always on the side of the ants and not on that of humans. Exaggeration, of course, but in all this excitement, with the baby crying, I agreed too, and if I'd laid hands on Signor Baudino then I couldn't say what I'd have done to him either.

The warm oil got the ant out; the baby, half stunned with crying, took up a celluloid toy, waved it about, sucked it and decided to forget us. I, too, felt the same need to be on my own and relax my nerves, but the women were still continuing their diatribe against Baudino, and they told my wife that he could probably be found in an enclosure nearby, where he had his warehouse. My wife exclaimed: " Ah, I'll go and see him, yes, go and see him and give him what he deserves! "

Then they formed a small procession, with my wife at the head and I, naturally, beside her, without giving any opinion on the usefulness of the undertaking, and other women who had incited my wife following and sometimes overtaking her to show her the way. The Signora Claudia offered to hold the baby and waved to us from the gate; I realised later that the Signora Aglaura was not with us either, although she had declared herself to be one of Baudino's most violent enemies, but we were accompanied by a little group of women we had not seen before. We went along a sort of courtyard road, flanked by wooden hovels, hen coops and vegetable gardens half full of rubbish. One or two of the women, in spite of all they'd said, stopped when they got to their own homes, stood on the threshold excitedly pointing out our direction, then retired inside calling to the dirty children playing on the ground, or disappeared to feed the chickens. Only a couple of women followed us as far as Baudino's enclosure; but when the door opened after heavy knocks by my wife we found that she and I were the only ones to go in, though we felt ourselves followed by the other women's eyes from windows or hen coops; they seemed to be continuing to incite us, but in very low voices and without showing themselves at all.

The ant-man was in the middle of his warehouse, a shack three-quarters destroyed, to whose one surviving wooden wall was tacked a yellow notice with letters a foot and a half long: " Argentine Ant Control Corporation." Lying all round were piles of those dishes for molasses and tins and bottles of every description, all in a sort of rubbish heap full of bits of paper with fish remains and other refuse, so that it immediately occurred to one that this was the source of all the ants of the area. Signor Baudino stood in front of us half smiling in an irritating questioning way, showing the gaps in his teeth.

" You," my wife attacked him, recovering herself after a moment of hesitation. " You should be ashamed of yourself! Why d'you come to our house and dirty everything and let the baby get an ant in his ear with your molasses."

She had her fists under his face, and Signor Baudino, without ceasing to give that decayed-looking smile of his, made the movements of a wild animal trying to keep its escape open, at the same time shrugging his shoulders and glancing and winking around to me, since there was no one else in sight, as if to say: "She's cracked." But his voice only uttered generalities and soft denials like: " No . . . No . . . Of course not."

" Why does everyone say that you give the ants a tonic instead of poisoning them? " shouted my wife, as he slipped out of the door into the road with my wife following him and screaming abuse. Now the shrugging and winking of Signor Baudino were addressed to the women of the surrounding hovels, and it seemed to me that they were playing some kind of double game, agreeing to be witnesses for him that my wife was insulting him; and yet when my wife looked at them they incited her, with sharp little jerks of the head and movements of the brooms, to attack the ant-man. I did not intervene; what could I have done? I certainly did not want to lay hands on the little man, as my wife's fury with him was already roused enough; nor could I try and moderate it, as I did not want to defend Baudino. At last my wife in another burst of anger cried: "You've done my baby harm!" grasped him by his collar and shook him hard.

I was just about to throw myself on them and separate them; but without touching her, he twisted round with movements that were becoming more and more ant-like, until he managed to break away. Then he went off with a clumsy, running step, stopped, pulled himself together, and went on again, still shrugging his shoulders and muttering phrases like: "But what behaviour . . . But who . . ." and making a gesture as if to say "She's crazy," to the people in the nearby hovels. From those people, the moment my wife threw herself on him, there rose an indistinct but confused mutter which stopped as soon as the man freed himself, then started up again in phrases not so much of protest and threat as of complaint and almost of supplication for sympathy, shouted out as if they were proud proclamations. "The ants are eating us alive . . . Ants in the bed, ants in the dishes, ants every day, ants every night. We've little enough to eat anyway and have to feed them too. . . ."

I had taken my wife by the arm. She was still shaking her fist every now and again and shouting: "It's not ended yet! We know who is swindling whom! We know whom to thank!" and other threatening phrases which did not echo back, as the windows and doors of the hovels on our path closed again, and the inhabitants returned to their wretched lives with the ants.

So it was a sad return, as could have been foreseen. But what had particularly disappointed me was the way those women had behaved. I swore I'd never go round complaining about ants again in my life. I longed to shut myself up in silent tortured pride like the Signora Mauro—but she was rich and we were poor. I had not yet found any solution to how we could go on living in these parts; and it seemed to me that none of the people here, who seemed so superior a short time ago, had found it, or were even on the way to finding it either.

We reached home; the baby was sucking his toy. My wife sat down on a chair. I looked at the ant-infested field and hedges, and beyond them at the cloud of insect powder rising from Signor Reginaudo's garden; and to the right there was the shady silence of the captain's garden, with that continuous dripping of his victims. This was my new home. I took my wife and child and said: " Let's go for a walk, let's go down to the sea."

It was evening. We went along alleys and streets of steps. The sun beat down on a sharp corner of the old town, on grey, porous stone, with lime-washed cornices to the windows and roofs green with moss. The town inside opened like a fan, undulating over slopes and hills, and the space between was full of limpid air, copper-coloured at this hour. Our child was turning round in amazement at everything and we had to pretend to take part in his marvelling; it was a way of bringing us together, of reminding us of the smooth flavour that life has at moments, and of reconciling us to the passing days.

We met old women balancing great baskets resting on head-pads, walking immobile with straight backs and lowered eyes; and in a nuns' garden a group of sewing girls ran along a railing to see a toad in a basin and said: " How awful! "; and behind an iron gate, under the wistaria, some young girls dressed in white were throwing a beach ball to and fro with a blind man; and a half naked youth with a beard and hair down to his shoulders was gathering Indian figs from an old cactus with a forked stick; and sad and spectacled children were making soap bubbles at the window of a rich house; it was the hour when the bell sounded in the old folks' home and they began climbing up the steps, one behind the other with their sticks, their straw hats on their heads, each talking to himself; and then there were two telephone workers, and one was holding a ladder and saying to the other on the pole: "Come on down, time's up, we'll finish the job to-morrow."

And so we reached the port and the sea. There was also a line of palm trees and some stone benches. My wife and I sat down and the baby was quiet. My wife said: "There are no ants here." I replied: "And there's a fresh wind; it's pleasant."

The sea beat to and fro against the rocks of the mole, making the fishing-boats sway, and men with dark skins were filling them with red nets and lobster pots for the evening's fishing. The water was calm, with just a slight continual change of colour, blue and black, darker farthest away. I thought of the expanses of water like this, of the infinite grains of soft sand down there at the bottom of the sea where the currents leave white shells washed clean by the waves.

THE END